To Jill
love
x x x
July 1993
Huby .

D1742543

FLORENCE AVENUE

BY THE SAME AUTHOR:

THE LEAST AND VILEST THINGS

PELICAN RISING

ENOUGH BLUE SKY

EVERYTHING IN THE GARDEN

FLORENCE AVENUE

A NOVEL

by

ELIZABETH NORTH

Elizabeth North

LONDON
VICTOR GOLLANCZ LTD
1979

© Elizabeth North 1979

ISBN 0 575 02680 4

MADE AND PRINTED IN GREAT BRITAIN BY
THE GARDEN CITY PRESS LIMITED
LETCHWORTH, HERTFORDSHIRE
SG6 1JS

For John and Jean

FLORENCE AVENUE

Sunday

The wider purpose of events escapes me often until later,
and things which turn out to have vital ends occur and pass
me by. For instance, there we were this evening, visiting our
close friends Pru and Gerry and it had been a weekend of
some note and things of some import had been discussed,
and while I mused upon these things I found myself diverted
by the trivia of their garden.

You could not have asked for a finer, balmier evening. A
hot day had preceded it. The sun was sinking over the hayfield which abuts their lawn and shining on their lovely long
low home of Yorkshire stone and still just falling on the
terrace where we sat with ice-cold cocktails in deep green
tumblers. Around us lay the fields and rolling country of
North Yorkshire. We felt at peace, in friendship and a touch
élite. It's nice sometimes to feel one's present at a search for
answers to the problems which have nagged at western culture
all through recent history, even if the thread of argument is
hard to follow on the whole.

I had got up and wandered to a nearby border, no doubt
intended as herbaceous. Unlike so many of us these days,
Gerry and Pru have made no attempt to become self-sufficient
by growing vegetables. They had, I admit, a token potato
plant in their rockery, but I took this to be an accidental
growth—sprouting from some relic maybe dropped by Pru,
who can be absent-minded when preparing vegetables. She
claims a planting, which it is not worth my while to question,
so I tell myself she is confused, as novelist, from time to time
with fact and fiction.

As I was saying, on this lovely sunlit evening with the hills
of Yorkshire at our backs and stretching up to the Dales at

north and west, we had sat in some contentment and the mood was one in which I could get up and leave the circle of white wicker chairs and examine the flowerbeds. The earth had recently been turned and thin stalks of couch-grass were beginning to emerge between small clumps of flowering plants. I knelt in my long cheesecloth skirt and began to pull these out and make a little pile of earthy roots on the neatly sliced lawn-edge.

Behind me they were talking still—Joel, my husband, Gerry and Pru, our friends. They talked about our little world of art, our plans and hopes and questions for a way ahead. And Gerry had been groping ever since the early afternoon to find the way ahead. He's always groping for a way ahead, and Joel, a good and caring friend to him, was saying that it all depended on the old conundrum—is it possible to have good life and good art too? And Bob, an old friend who'd arrived the day before, was with them too, or so I thought. I'll get to where Bob was, in fact, quite soon.

Now Joel and I do not grow flowers. Our life is aimed at providence these days. I've no regrets at that, but all the same my work has veered of recent years to what must be described as nature poetry. And so I visit public gardens, florists with a notebook, write down close-up observations. As far as I'm concerned, the details matter, even though as I have mentioned, broader issues tend to slip my grasp.

It must be that the others feel more bound up in events. They sometimes seem to think they'll change the world, and it is not for me to tell them that I cannot see their words can shift the irreducibilities. I have to tell myself that speculations of the kind they make are like the prayers of monks and nuns, to no apparent end, the idea being that a fund of prayer will somehow stock a basically uncaring universe with good—or rather thoughts of good.

But even so, it was with some relief I left the terrace and became absorbed in pulling couch-grass fronds from good soft earth. And they indulged my absence, believing me perhaps to be conjuring up another nature poem, so they let me

10

be. But at this point I was surprised to feel a hand upon my waist, descending to my buttocks.

At first, believing this was Joel, I made no move, but then I heard his voice, a long way back beside the house. It must be Bob, I thought, our friend who lives down south but who has been away from all of us for years and does not realise that we are now all reformed and steady members of society.

I was a little miffed with Bob. He could have made the move more tactfully, not to say less furtively. I will not say he only has to ask. But as it was, I felt that he was taking an unfair advantage of me. No doubt he can remember that my early work was rife with sexual innuendo and he still believes life follows art as we all did way back.

While thinking what to do about his straying hand I went on pulling bits of couch-grass up until there were no more within my reach. But all the same I realised that by staying in this posture, passive, kneeling, he would assume I welcomed such a crude approach.

Poor Bob, he burns with passion for a mistress he has lost, and those of us who have rewarding sexual partners should feel sorry for him, I am sure. However, it must be said he is the only man against whom I have ever had to warn my daughter.

"I think," I said, "I'll have to move, if you don't mind."
His hand stayed still.
"I think we may be going in for dinner soon," I said.

He made no move. It had occurred to me that Joel might see, and while he's very seldom jealous, he would rise in anger if he thought I was the slightest bit discomfited. However, since he had been well content all day, I was loth to call upon him for assistance.

Meanwhile the situation apropos of Bob was pressing. If I moved back against his hand, it would suggest a measure of enjoyment. And yet ahead of me were several yards of border, catmint, pinks, carnations and a rather prickly shrub I think is called mahonia. The smell of catmint wafted up to me. I like to be this close to nature, but, trapped as I was,

11

I could not pay attention to the details of the leaves and earth.

My movement forward was encumbered also by my skirt of ankle length. I had to rise a little to release a fold of this from underneath my knee. But after that I gently crawled across the border as if this was a simple thing to do. I stood up, more or less unscathed, and brushed my skirt from crumbs of soil and shreds of leaf and looked around. And Bob had gone.

I bent once more and gathered up the couch-grass strands. I moved towards the low stone wall which ends the garden, dropped the weeds into the hayfield, recently mown, had a sniff of fragrance here and then rejoined the others on the terrace. Their heads were still in sun, their feet in shade, stones dark, the sun having moved down in the sky towards the furthest western rolling hill in sight. I looked across at them.

Gerry cut his hair in 1975, Joel in 1976. Joel had thought of cutting his in 1975 as well, but did not wish to seem to be imitating Gerry. We both agree that one must be individual and make one's decisions in the matter of significant moves.

Bob's hair is still below his ears. It is both thin and greasy and one can't help thinking that this may put off some women he pursues. It's not for me, however, to advise him. He might go off and have his hair cut, then return believing I'd be ready for him.

I am not drawn to Bob. I'm only drawn to Joel. Except on rare occasions when we have selective orgies, I give myself to no one else. Joel's skin is very white and burns. I'd made him wear his hat—a broad-brimmed Panama I bought for him. It makes him look distinguished, hides his baldness, and his beard gets bleached around the edges in the summer time. And all in white, which suits him very well, he looked today a bit like pictures I have seen of D. H. Lawrence visiting Lady Ottoline Morrell.

"Hello, my precious jewel," Joel reached his hand to me.

"Hullo, my darling heart," I said and put my hand in his and asked what they had been discussing since I left.

12

"The Grassington Award," he said.

"I thought it was good life/good art," I said. I held my glass and Pru bent down to fill it with Campari, and she added soda. Her arms were brown. She wore a sleeveless cotton top. Her breasts were loose, her bosom firm for someone late-ish in her forties. I felt Joel flinch and cross his legs. He never fails to be intensely moved by any sensual gesture. But he is not, I hasten to add, like Bob. Joel looks and loves and is extremely well contained. I hope that, should these words be read at any time by people who know Joel, they will not say, "Ah ha! So that is what she thought!"

No, Joel is good. He is a good man and believes in good. I rather think he is the only one of us to go so far as to acknowledge it as a true and undeniable abstract. His poems used to throb with fleshy images. Less so now. They rather thrum with moral questiness.

I held his hand and my Campari to the sun. "So who will win the Grassington Award?" I said.

And Gerry said: "It will be Joel. His day is coming now. His voice will ring across the wastes."

And it is true to say we have high hopes of Joel's most recent work, in which he poses questions such as, 'Who is fit to judge?' 'Who is fit to hold responsibility?' and 'Have we passed the buck to younger people when they were not ready for it?' The title of this poem *Children, Animals and Idiots* is a phrase he learned when doing Ethics at an evening class, and is a term describing that class of beings for whom decisions must be made.

The words which Gerry spoke were not untinged with bitterness. His wicker chair creaked under him. He is a stocky man, aggressive, and as Pru so often laments to me, he is in mid-life crisis now. He is an ex-iconoclast and used to lead. He did most things before most people. He grew his hair long first, joined an Encounter Group first, read McLuhan and R. D. Laing first, went on the road first, took mistresses first, was divorced first, and conversely, as already mentioned, was the first to have his hair cut short, remove his single ear-ring, criticise Encounter Groups, remarry and begin to sell the Beatles short and say that Monty Python wasn't funny after all.

"Oh come on, Gerry, don't be sad," I said, but spoke half-heartedly. My mind was full of Joel. He's not in mid-life crisis yet, or maybe he is on the lower slopes of it. I watch for signs, however, and it's true to say his vision's very dire about the world he sees about him, hating as he does the loudest sounds and brightest plastic colours. I know that it is not unusual to deplore vulgarity, but I think Joel minds it more than most. It blights his life but fuels his work. Of all the members of New Pathways Poetry Group, of which we are (I do not boast) the centrepiece, he is most likely to receive the Grassington Award.

The garden rises just beyond the terrace and the grass there is well mown, shrubs neatly, roundly shaped. Syringa bloomed and gave exotic scent. Pru's crystal tumblers, lemon slices, parsley florets floating in the deep blue jug of Pimms. I felt exclusive once again; the scene around was as might be portrayed in an advertisement. I held up my Campari to the sky to see if that blue sky would turn the rose pink liquid, as it bubbled, to a mauve, and thought: 'Campari held against the evening sky turns mauve'. That is not very promising maybe, but never mind. I stretched and sniffed the evening air instead and breathed in smells of new-mown hay and smoke from Pru's cigar.

I like a spacious place to eat. I need space either side of me, am too affected by a person's presence to sit close and carry on a normal conversation. Tonight this dining-room was right for summer, cool stone floor and marble table. You have to keep your elbows off it in the winter. The table, circular, a multi-coloured art nouveau lamp hung low.

The food, although deep frozen, cooked by someone else and served up hastily by Pru, was very good. But rather rich. The salmon mousse and coq au vin was greatly to my taste, but Joel just toyed with it. From time to time he turns his face against all hedonism. He is not greedy anyway.

Pru seldom cooks herself. She needs the time to work, of course. She's started on her second novel *See-Through Man*, but really she's rejected all domestic roles these days. Her feminist views are strong and so are mine, but I believe in the power of the provider and the prime of place behind the stove, or if you like, the iron fist in the oven glove. I have discovered that the time of meals directs the pace of life, and would not wish for more control than that.

Poor Pru. I feel for her. She is ambitious for a life of literature which might well take off to circles far away beyond the confines of ourselves and even Gerry, and she finds it hard to pander to his waywardness. She could go far. Unlike myself she has no children who might hamper her. Although she claims this lack could well affect her writing in the end. I try to help her in this matter, and give her hints about the role of mother. The childbirth scene in *Counterpunch*, which got much praise, was word for word—or push for push—my own expulsion of my daughter Clo.

The wine tonight was deep and red. I think the conversation centred round the poem Gerry's entered for the Grassington Award, and parts of which he'd read aloud when first we came. In fact he'd read it twice. I hadn't listened much, although it seemed to be upon a subject he had used before. Set in his home town Doncaster, it was about, I think, the struggle of a miner's lad to reach a better land and time, a longish poem on the whole. The theme was that of struggle. He claimed for it that there was nowhere in *Pit Lad* a sense of knocking or complaint, in accordance with his recent change of purpose.

Bob had been quiet. I sensed resentment from him. I had let him down perhaps. He is a stocky little Yorkshire man, the only one of us apart from Gerry who is native to this place. But he has missed out on our recent goings-on. He interrupted Gerry at this point: "Oh no, old lad, we can't have this. I mean to say, where's all the protest? Where's

15

the hate and blood and snot and all the gritty bits you used to write about?"

There was a little pause and several people cleared their throats. Someone—I think it may have been Joel—spoke out about the need for change in art, new attitudes, new trends. Someone may even have spoken in the terms of new morality. And Bob said: "Numerality? What's that got to do with it?"

"It's two words, Bob, and things have changed," I said.

Bob looked at me. "I've noticed. Aye, I've noticed. Well, you may be right. It may be new bandwagon so no doubt you'll want to jump on it. It makes you sound like bleeding Tories, if you want to know!"

A silence followed. Gerry put his chin in his left hand, picked up a piece of bread and wiped it all around his plate. He thinks that actions of this kind establish him as of true working-class origins, but Joel, who comes from genuinely down-trodden people, claims that not a lot of that goes on, and I who come from middle-class have seen it done in many kinds of home, and Pru, who comes from upper class, has often said her father did it all the time. I wish that Gerry would just wipe his plate with bread because the sauce was good and claim no sociological causes for the action.

With a name like McLeHose his claim to low birth must be weakened. He may have had bone broth, it's true. I think his family fell on hard times in the 1930s' slump, but once, when driving into Doncaster with him, he pointed out to us the street in which he lived, and there were houses well set back, detached and some with brass plates by their doors.

Pru rose and shook her hair and went to fetch the baked Alaska. Joel told a story about an Irishman he'd heard at work, and then when Gerry still was silent, he told another one about a Pole. Joel's contribution is to distance all the anguish people feel, with humour. Then he told another story about an Italian in Australia. But Gerry took a pair of shaded glasses out of the pocket of his shirt and put them on.

He has been well known in his time, not great perhaps and never quite a name to conjure with. A name unfortunately

16

forgotten now and never quite a household word. To those who've heard the name of McLeHose I apologise, and to those who have slim volumes of his work on shelves, the small space that they take up is not wasted. He sat there, Gerry did, and said: "Ah, so I'm finished. Perhaps I will not make the short-list even, and like Monica I will accept a back seat now and be content with just a page or two in very little magazines".

He was referring to our own *New Pathways* which I edit and which has a not unreasonable circulation. I was about to rise in its defence and in my own. I have had poems printed elsewhere too—*Fem Press* for one. But Joel who senses every minor tremor in my usual implacability, was kicking me beneath the table by that time. And Pru returned and turned to Bob and quizzed him on his life in the metropolis. She tends to fear we are provincial in our attitudes and likes to pick up gossip from those places where it's possible they are more avant garde. But Bob was not expansive on the matter. He lives in Teddington and works in Twickenham and talked about the greenhouse he was building.

Pru yawned and after that the party rather fell apart. Bob, Pru and I played Scrabble. Joel wandered in the garden ill at ease. But Gerry sat indoors, his earphones on, and listened to some hi-fi birdsong he recorded in the Dales. He has been down a pit, it's true. He was a Bevan Boy in 1949 instead of doing National Service. He draws on that for writing, but his income comes from business and he runs a printing firm. There was a photo of him in the *Yorkshire Post* last year. The title under it read 'Printer/Poet'. There he was in leather jacket and cravat with shooting-stick and workman's cap, chin-up, windblown and elemental. He does not talk about his business much. I understand they print receipts and invoice forms, although each year he rolls his sleeves up, sets his presses to the task of bringing out *New Pathways*.

The sky above us as we drove towards our home was colourless with stars, but moonlit, clear. The air was cool. I'd won at Scrabble and I felt content in spite of what had gone before. And Joel seemed soothed from walking in the garden on his own. He seemed approachable. I watched him with much love.

Our car is old. Joel goes to classes now to learn about its maintenance. We have gone further, to my mind, in self-sufficiency than almost anyone we know. And people marvelled rather when we recently announced that Joel had given up his last job as a civil service clerk and was training as an apprentice joiner now and going to building college down in Leeds. Our little home is now a feast of all his skill, of polished oak and pine and red mahogany.

We drove there on a flat and straight wide grass-verged road in moonlight, headed south along this ridge of hills. I saw the shape of trees and thought about the colour of the trees which is not black at night, but something dark. I should not worry quite so much about the colour of the things I see. I should search rather for other ways of describing day and night.

I also needed to draw close to Joel: "I wish you could *both* win the Grassington Award," I said, thus showing Joel that while I felt compassion for the state of Gerry's ego, I knew that he himself deserved to win. He touched my hand and said: "Well, why not you as well?"

My entry this year is an ode, revised. I wrote it for my daughter, Clo, some years ago. I tried so hard to stick to new ideas in this updated piece. I have not knocked a thing. I've rather knocked myself out to be constructive and to make a point. I cannot quite remember what the point exactly is. The most that I can hope for is 'commended' or perhaps an uncommended mention. The competition will be judged next Saturday.

I sometimes say to Joel: "Why can't we stay the way we were, assume the literary inheritance which was ours, be truly cynical, decadent, and watch it all fall down. And let it fall so far that those who come to follow us will hold their hands in horror and react with much more built-in fervour than we possibly can have?"

18

And Joel says: "Fie!" and "Fie for shame!" and drives on in the night.

We'll go there up to Grassington on Saturday and we'll listen while the poems which have won are read out by the winners. I have to say that Gerry hasn't won for four years now. The open competition is so open now that last year a poet living in Bratislava won; the year before the winner came from Guernsey. Gerry did come second then and third the year before.

I called my entry *Ode to my Daughter on her Sixteenth Birthday*, but I feel it's not my own true voice that speaks in it. I have compared the growing girl to growing trees. The only line I feel is worthy of award of any kind is 'You are greenstick still'.

The truth about Clo's sixteenth birthday is that she got cards from all her friends with captions like: 'At last! At last!', 'The hour has come!' and 'May I be the first?'

I sensed Joel's mood was one of disengagement from myself, and said: "Oh well—we all feel guilty if an evening has been fraught, but then the moonlight's bright, the temperature is absolutely right, we are together and for now this minute we do have good life anyway, it might be said. . ."

"Forget all else, you mean?"

"Life's mixed, for heavens' sake. It can't be otherwise."

The trees flashed past, the moon behind, a million shadows as a backdrop to his gentle, sad and disillusioned face. He hates my too-consistent relish of the yins and yangs of everything.

Our house is on the edge of town. At the back it overlooks some playing fields. We chose it very carefully. It had not to be grand by any means. We were to live most simply, unpretentiously, anonymously. Craftsmen-poets, we wished to share the street with craftsmen-plumbers, decorators, builders, and if necessary, salesmen and clerks like Joel had been, although we would prefer the artisans.

Our house looks ordinary from the outside. Semi-detached

19

and pebble-dashed, garden on three sides, stake fence surrounds and mostly we grow vegetables. The potatoes in the front are the only thing which makes our house look different from the others in the street.

We parked the car on the concrete patch outside the garage and we kissed inside it. Then we went indoors. Our house, inside, I think is rather different from the others in the street. We have knocked through—not one partition of the ground floor of our house, but all of them, so that at street level it is one huge room—well, not that huge—and painted glowing dark translucent green, lightened here and there with white and full of paintings given us by people in the visual arts. Our long downstairs room is a feast of greenery with ferns and trailing tradescantia and many richly textured growing things. Nothing flowering because flowers move me less than leaves. Flowers die fast and leaves survive. I started off a poem with that line I've just remembered, but I think I never finished it.

Our floor is pale and sanded varnished wood. It is a very pleasant room and we have worked to make it so, had many magic moments of togetherness and common purpose here when choosing things and painting walls and hanging pictures up.

Our young friend Bruce got up as we came in. He had been watching television. He wants to be a film director, Bruce, and stayed behind tonight to be with my son Jamie. At thirteen Jamie's old enough to be here on his own, but it was nice to think Bruce stayed with him. Perhaps Bruce felt he owed us that. He's very little trouble, though, and with us at the moment since a rift took place quite recently between him and his friend Theresa.

He got up as we came in, stretched and shook his short blond hair. He is from Parramatta, Sydney, Australia. "Hullo, folks! How did it go?" and I said "Fine", and asked him if it had gone well here. I also asked him if Clo had come in as yet. Clo's been away for several days—in fact about a week,

I think. She's with her lover and they went to watch the summer solstice pass at somewhere like Stonehenge, but should be back by now. Although she stays with Maurice at his flat for most weekends, she comes home Sunday evenings to get her books for school on Monday.

No, Clo had not come back, but Jamie'd gone to bed an hour ago. I checked my watch. Eleven-thirty was a little late. He's off to camp tomorrow morning very early.

I asked Bruce if he'd watered the courgettes, the sweetcorn, the tomatoes and he said he had. He is obliging and I'll miss him if he does return in due course to Theresa, though she yearns for him I know. And then I wandered to our kitchen end. A rich display of Joel's new craft is here. Every surface, cupboard door and even some interiors are lined with offcuts of teak, pine or mahogany. I sometimes think that Joel should specialise eventually in marquetry. The place was neat. Bruce tidies well and is meticulous.

Joel went upstairs and fell asleep upon our big brass bed. I had not thought he was so tired. I lay and watched him, felt apart from him again and longed to rouse him, touch his back. I thought about a poem which I might soon write about two people making love entwined like columbines. No, not like columbines. What else in nature gets entwined?

I made some notes and listened for Clo's footsteps in the road. There's emptiness when she is not about. The weekend has been most eventful on the whole, shot through with thoughts about a letter which arrived on Saturday. The stamp was French. The letter read:

Dear Monica,
    You may be quite surprised to know that after all these years I am about to be re-married. I am surprised myself in many ways. Françoise is 32, RC of course, but not too strict. We will be married at the Maire, Argelès-sur-Mer, in late July.

I read this letter in the garden early Saturday. James Crossley,

21

my ex-husband, wrote from Perpignan. I *was* surprised. Last time I heard from James he was in Ethiopia. I looked again: 're-married' shifted on the flimsy airmail paper and appeared as 're-interred'.

The main thing is I'd like the children to be there. At least it seems they can be offered something from this side apart from money. Perhaps they could stay on a while. Françoise has a small apartment. I don't know if you had some summer plans or not . . .

The first thing was I wondered if I could get both the children there in time. For Jamie, as I mentioned, was about to go to camp, and Clo had not been seen for several days. But late July, depending on how late in July he meant, was several weeks away.

I fetched my glasses, read the letter properly. Then Joel came down. I showed it to him and I told him that I didn't know exactly how I felt about the news. I knew that I was moved but could not say which way. In fact Joel made a fuss of me all day, kept patting me from time to time and saying things like now we would be well and truly married, which we have been now for several years. And Bruce kept making jokes like, "Break a tube of Fosters, Bruce". He calls Joel Bruce—another joke.

And Jamie said he thought that Perpignan was down in Roussillon which part of France had goodish wine. Could he wear his best new hacking jacket to the wedding, but he didn't want to be too hot.

I will not say this news pressed on my mind the weekend through, but it's been in the background of my thoughts and needs a mention here. I plan to write my early life as well as this, the record of my present one. And James comes into both inevitably.

We did have something he and I maybe when Clo was born. We christened her Clarissa which was very classy then.

22

And by the time a lot of people copied us and called their little girls Clarissa, I had altered it to Clo. We had a classy suburb house as well, but when James left and said he needed freedom to explore the world, I wasn't surprised. I was quite glad in fact. It meant that I could marry Joel.

Monday: a.m.

Perhaps, I wondered late last night, if Joel was silent, less approachable because, although he'd patted me and been affectionate all Saturday, the news from James had cast him down. Perhaps his statement: "Now we're truly wed" had come right home to him by then. Perhaps it was a blow and not a comfort to him.

And thus it was in fairly gloomy frame of mind I set out very early on today to drive my son to camp, or rather drive him to the station. He looked so frail there on the platform with a dozen other boys. His rucksack looked too big for him. He did not kiss me when I said good-bye, permitted me to kiss him though.

At breakfast he'd been all dressed up to go, but in that hacking jacket, best beige needlecords and blue silk tie. "Oh, not your best clothes, darling. Surely your tracksuit and your trainers would be best!" He cried into his Weetabix. Then Bruce came down and slapped him on the back: "Hi, superboy!" and Jamie cried again.

On the way down to the station few words passed between us. I tried to formulate a thought that boys who like good wine and nice silk ties and whose only other interest seems to be in outer space, should be beyond the shedding of so many tears this early in the morning, shouldn't they? And he was only going for a week, and missing school to boot.

I thought of Joel again, for it was his ascetic leanings prompted this departure from the norm in Jamie's life. And after all the camp looked nice enough. The brochure illustrated it as on a sloping sward, tall pines, a lake-edge site. We only chose it after much consideration. "It will be lovely in the Lakes," I said with a briskness which I did not feel.

Jamie looked down at his tracksuit and his training shoes with some disgust. I said: "You know it said you shouldn't take best clothes."

"I read the brochure too, you know," he said with tearful vehemence. I'm still amazed from time to time that, though I have been rather stern with him for several years, he manages to make me feel put down. I rallied though. "Experience like this," I said, "can teach us all the things that we can do without."

"Or make us want them even more."

I felt like touching Jamie's hair, but knew that this would be unwise. His hair is blond and silky and must always stay the way his own self-image has decreed. His face is soft and girlish still. He could just do with losing weight maybe. I was put in mind of a Horace Ode which Joel translated once. It went like this:

So let the young boy smiling
Learn his hardship in the Roman way.
And sharpened thus,
With horse and spear deter wild Parthians.

The image of my son in shortish toga, vaulting on a horse and managing a spear as well with ease, so moved me that I had to put my brisk tone on again: "It will be lovely in the Lakes," I said.

"You can't be sure of that."

He has his father's doubt of things unknown. That doubt which took his father round the world to prove that things he hadn't seen existed, I suppose. That trip which ended just the other day at Perpignan. It would be very hot down there in late July. I wondered if I would get Jamie something new and cool to wear, a denim suit maybe. . .

But here today—the grip of early morning mist. The buildings of our town are mostly dark and looming eighteenth-century stone and touched by sooty air from down-wind wool and factory towns. But here and there they have been cleaned and have a honey glow.

25

"About the camp. Just take it in your stride," I said to Jamie, which were Joel's own words last night.

"I wonder how he'd take it in his stride," said Jamie in the car.

"Do you mean Joel?"

"I do mean Joel."

I could not cross my heart and say I thought that Joel would take it in his stride. Instead I said: "I'll feed the goldfish for you all this week," and he said nothing, knowing, as we both knew, that I always feed the goldfish anyway. "And when you're home again we'll open up that first new batch of turnip wine. . ."

"Big deal," said Jamie.

And I drove home blinking tears away. And found Bruce still around. He sat there on our only garden chair and read the *Guardian*, smoked his pipe and hoped, I think, to get some sun on him, although as far as I could see the mist might hang around all day. He likes fresh air, but otherwise he doesn't do the things Australians are said to do—play cricket, take a lot of exercise. He has not been as useful in the case of Jamie as he might have been. I felt less warmly to him, sorry for his girlfriend too. She's very broken-hearted, rings up often asking for him.

"Will Bruce be here when I get back?" said Jamie just before he caught the train.

"Oh, heaven knows," I said.

"Theresa's preying on his mind."

"I'm not surprised. And so she should."

"It isn't fair on Bruce."

"And how do you think Theresa feels?"

"I hadn't thought of that."

"Well, you must think of things like that." I am surprised at Jamie sometimes. Carefully brought up to cook and sew as much as play with trains and Action Man, he still shows symptoms of a sexist kind. And now to send him off to camp with boys alone! "What will it do to him?" I said when running into Joel in bed.

26

Joel sleepily sat up and stretched a hand to reach his spectacles. He quoted Horace once again: "Unwarlike youths, like timid sheep, get hit behind the knees." I put his glasses on for him and said, "Oh darling, that's not fair. I mean you hated National Service, didn't you?"

"Well, blanket stores are boring at the best of times, but I could fight if needed now", and he predicted that within a day or two we'd get a postcard from the lakeside camp with message: 'A.O.K. am having smashing time.'

"I can't see that," I said and sniffed and went to tidy Jamie's room. I hung discarded clothes on hangers, made the bed, tried not to look at pictures of him as a little boy. But stepped upon a plastic model of a spaceship which was on the floor. It cracked. I cried again. It is the only Airfix model he has ever finished.

When Joel had gone to college, Bruce as well, I stood outside and looked across the recreation ground where there are swings and metal climbing frames and slides, a kind of roundabout which children stand upon and scoot around. We partly chose the house for all that exercising fun, for Jamie when he was a few years younger. I can't say that he's ever used it all that much.

Clo says I'm much too hard on Jamie and she disapproved of plans for sending him to camp. "To think what things I did at that age too!" she said.

"It happens that I've changed my view," I said, "I used to think the natural way was right. I now see that the nurtured way is possibly . . ."

"But he was nine at least before you changed your mind. It must be so confusing . . ."

"And to think I brought you up to appreciate the contrasts . . ."

"Yeah, well, maybe, but there are contrasts and there's contrasts. Maurice says that anyhow the universe is all one thing . . ."

"Well, Maurice *would* . . ."

"I *knew* you didn't like him."

"Clo! Of course I like him . . . well, I mean . . ."

"He knows it. He can sense it. He can sense the tiniest blip of hatred on the surface of . . ."

"I know he's very sensitive."

"He's drawn a picture of the universe, symbolic-like, a bit. It's all in mauve felt pen."

"Come on, Clo. Anyone can colour in the universe in all one shade. It's not like you to . . ."

"I don't think you have any idea just how fucked up people's minds can get by always being told about the contradictions and the yin and yang. I honestly believe that I knew how to spell yin and yang before I could spell cat. And have you thought that, even if the universe isn't all in mauve felt pen, it might be nice to think it was?"

I couldn't fault her reasoning on that. She needs some comfort of the mental kind. She has been disillusioned now for quite some years. She is a sad leftover from the time, not so many years ago, when it seemed the revolution was at hand. Not that she aimed to have a part in it, but thought the hungry would pervade the streets and she, with small cool hands, would lead them to her place and give them soup and bathe their brows.

A card I had from Clo the other day, a picture of Stonehenge:

A super solstice here and crowds of people and I had my rucksack stolen. It had a hole in it. Heaps and tons and enormous piles of love to all.

I wasn't that surprised about the rucksack. Clo's prone to losing things like that. It's not that she has disregard for property, but rather that she would believe that someone needed something very badly if they went as far as taking it from her.

Jamie, looking at the card, said: "Do you think she'll marry Maurice in the end?"

I said: "Clo's much too young to settle down."

"You married very young you always say."

"One did in those days . . . *now* we know."

I don't know where he gets ideas of early marriage from. Perhaps from television, since the only books he reads are sci-fi magazines and wine trade journals which he gets from his friend Mark whose father manages the off-licence down on Phyllis Road.

"There is an Arab boy proposed to her, you know."

"Oh really? Well. I don't think Clo . . ."

"He's from Iraq. His father's in the army there. He is important. He might ask us to Baghdad."

The train came in and Jamie stood there blinking in the second class, expressionless with one hand raised, his version of a wave perhaps.

Another card from Clo came early on last week. This time the Tor at Glastonbury. From this it will be clear that Maurice has an interest in astrology. The message read:

We've moved on here. M. rather low, says stars are bad for Joel. Mars in Cancer.

I hid this card from Joel. He angrily rejects astrology and I myself take little notice of the stars. In fact when Maurice said he'd chart my horoscope, no charge, I turned the offer down. It might be bad, the future, so I said, "No thank you, dear." Clo said, "He's very hurt. He thinks you don't believe in him."

"You tell him that it is because I think he'd get it right that I don't want to know. Don't tell him when my birthday is," I said.

"I think he knows. You had a party once."

"But not my *time* of birth. I'm not divulging that."

But Maurice hasn't spoken to me since I turned him down. He never speaks a lot in any case. Perhaps that is not fair. Let's say he's not effusive in his speech. I mean no doubt he speaks to Clo and I have seen him with her many times and seen his lips to move a lot.

Another card came Friday last. Another picture of the Tor at Glastonbury. "Have met amazing bloke. He makes guitars and things and lives in Cornwall. Maurice says stars bad for Daddy now. Jupiter in Capricorn", and this the day before the news from Perpignan.

I turn my face against foreboding thoughts. I like my life. I have my love from Joel, and even if he turned his back and slept last night, past records show that only days will pass before he needs the solace of my arms again. I also have my friends: there's Pru with whom I can discuss the realms of literature, the novel whither?—all that sort of thing, although we disagree on feministic principles. And then next door there are our neighbours, Ron and Barbara. They are affable and sound. He is a plumber, Ron, a most successful one. They've just come back from cruising in the Adriatic.

Although, as said, I like my life and relish Monday mornings with a day of work ahead, I could not help but feel a little apocalyptic on the whole. A brooding sense of worse to come, a lethargy which would not lift. I took a lemovite, a decongestant too, in case I had a summer cold.

But nothing stirred the heaviness. The mist, which we call North Sea fret, still hung around, although I felt the sun was just behind it somewhere. I lifted up the rush mats, threw them in the garden and I swept the floor. The dustbin echoed as I banged the lid and tried to find some promise in the day. I'd do some work and later I would chat to Barbara. Then Pru might come around, and Ron as well who comes in after work to tell us all about the place where he has worked each day, the bathroom fittings he's installed, the kind of tea or coffee given him.

Meanwhile I went upstairs to work upon my terza rima. Its theme is nature/nurture—"that old thing", as Pru would say, upon which I have mused until I am, to tell the truth, quite sick of it. The poem is concerned with growing of tomato plants from seed. It reads so far:

Is each seed destined as it touches soil
To thrive or not regardless of the care
With which we toil?

I put it on one side. I might go on with my 'campari held
against an evening sky turns mauve' idea. But that reminded
me of Maurice and his felt pen picture of the universe. I
looked out of the window and I hummed a bit and thought
of going round to Barbara for a cup of coffee, but I then sat
down and wrote another verse, referring to a plant of ours
which perished young:

Beside you unintended daisies where
We planted one like you in early spring,
No longer there.

That verse is very weak. I took my list of words to rhyme
with 'where', considered for a moment 'air' or, since the
tomato plant which died young had its share of care from us,
perhaps I'd fit in 'care'.

The sun does not come in this room until late afternoon.
Nor was there any sun as yet, and moisture cloaked the
roofs and gardens opposite. I could hear Barbara's auto-
washer thrumming, but I kept on looking at the terza rima.
Once Joel read me out a quote of Donne's:

The whole frame of a poem is the beating out of a piece
of gold, but the last clause is as the impression of a stamp
and that is it that makes it current.

Considering the terza rima with a yawn, I doubted if the
last clause would be anything. This poem must be positive;
it had to show that nurture—i.e. interference—was successful.
I thought of Clo who has had hardly any interference in her
life, and then of Jamie who has had a lot. And neither of
them has exactly flourished yet:

A gap of dried up earth, a ring
Of dust, a shrivelled stalk is all to show,
A shred of string.

31

I think I shed a tear, then blew my nose. For after all I've nurtured Clo as well. She is the product of my state of mind as she grew up. Inbred in her my views on early marriage, loss of independence, how to turn your back on anything that smacks of petty bourgeoisie, I think. I well remember how aged ten she wrote a letter of condolence to a cousin who had been persuaded into a career in chartered accountancy.

Still nothing came to help the terza rima on its way. Could observation help? Could close-up study of the garden and tomato plants wring out some truth? Could Barbara help? This neighbour—always ready for a chat, whose steady view of life, more primitive than mine perhaps, but none the less a reassuring presence who's across the fence at any time of day. I fetched my wide straw hat and took my pen and paper and I went outside. There busy noises of a Monday morning out along the backs and Barbara with her washing line and pegs and almost tribal instincts for the answers to our many problems of the day.

She always washes Monday, says it is a ritual she cannot miss and feels uneasy if she does. I heard her in the garden very near to me. I studied the tomato plant, appeared to be as deep in contemplation as I ever am, and did not turn my head.

She spoke first, Barbara did. She raised her voice: "Owt wrong, our Monica?" and called again, "Owt wrong?"

I knelt and made some notes about the texture of tomato plants and then some rhymes like 'nourish', 'flourish' and I thought of 'courage' too. And then called out, not looking up, that I was bothered with the yin and yang of things, dilemmas, contradictions and confusion of existence, and then because, although she's very sharp, I thought she might not understand the nature/nurture problem, I simply said there was a kind of emptiness about.

"Oh that!" said Barbara. "Well, Ron's been proper maungy too." I was concerned for Ron. He's usually so sound and full of comforting opinions. He reads from history books he gets sent in by post and often says that things today are no worse than they've ever been. We hadn't seen a lot of him since Friday, so I shouted out: "Poor Ron. What does it do for him?"

"It sends him to the Lamb and Flag bit more than other times," said Barbara. She's good to look at too, with crisp blonde curls and strong brown arms, long legs. She took a clothes peg from her mouth and pushed it firmly on the corner of a flowery sheet. Her tumbler-drier renders things bone dry, but all the same she feels she has not done her washing if she has not used the line. She pushed another token peg on to another token sheet. She often says that she was trained in washing by Ron's mother and she always thinks of that old cow on washing days: "I feel her up there checking that I do it like she showed me how."

I seized on that. It seemed to me that Barbara yet again had honed in on a nugget of amazing truth. "And do you sometimes think that gives you strength?" I said, "And do you sometimes think that having someone, even someone dead, who has a deep effect on actions still, does lend, in some possibly transcendent fashion, a moral structure to your life?"

She thought a bit and then said, "No."

"It could mean, couldn't it, ancestor worship in a way?" I said.

"You want to get Joel put you up a line," said Barbara and I sensed a coolness in her voice. She went inside. The flapping flowery sheets were in one corner of my eye and put me off my study of the plants. I was alarmed that she'd gone off like that. Joel is emphatic in his wish that we do not offend our neighbours. I'm less experienced than him and have not lived like this before, so close to others, cheek by jowl.

Her head appeared again between two sunflowers growing by the fence. "Your trouble is that Clo," she said.

"It was a bit more cosmic than just Clo," I said.

She disappeared again. I'd have to make it right. The trouble is that it is Ron and Barbara's silver wedding day on

33

Saturday, and it wouldn't do to spoil the atmosphere along this even-numbered side of Florence Avenue. Or further upset Joel, for he concerns himself, is anxious that our rather scrappy and haphazard lives may somehow mar, corrupt or otherwise affect the gilt-edged soundness of next door.

An idea came. I went to Barbara, took her glossy shopping catalogue and pointed out a garden frame I'd like. "What for?" she said, a little tight-lipped still.

"For our courgettes next year."

"You fill in form," she took a sheaf of papers from a drawer and put them on her kitchen table for me.

She was ironing now, some silky shirts of Ron's, and then the pale blue overalls he wears for work. "I bet you are excited about Saturday," I said.

"What's that?"

"Your silver wedding, isn't it?"

"Oh that!" she said, but offered me an After Eight—she had the packet just beside her as she ironed. I didn't say I thought she was on the bran diet now, but stayed and chatted to her for a while, discovered what the trouble was. Her Nicola, the daughter who is reading anthropology at Cambridge (Trinity—they do have girls there now), is going up in a balloon and may not make it for the silver wedding day.

"I know just how you feel," I said.

"You had your silver wedding then?"

"Well—no, in fact."

"I thought you wouldn't have."

I changed the subject, tactfully I thought, and said she should be very proud of Nicola. It isn't every girl from a Yorkshire comprehensive school who gets to be the secretary of the Cambridge University Balloon Club. And Barbara grunted several times and went on ironing in a walnut-fitted kitchen where brass handles shone.

I tried to write my early life today. Began: 'Born Isle of Wight' and wondered if I'd put the date or not, decided that it did not matter much, but left a space for it.

Born Isle of Wight. My father was a pilot. It was his speciality to guide ships past the Needles. He guided ocean liners, tankers, any large ships coming up the Solent aiming for Southampton. Usually he sailed with them from Cherbourg or Le Havre, having travelled there himself by channel steamer or another liner. He was away from home a lot. Simply in order to guide two ships per week past the Needles—the work of just an hour or two—he had to spend at least five days per week away from home.

I paused and sucked my biro. Ink came out. The sun had not got through the mist. The roofs across the road looked steely grey.

I'm five foot one and wear high heels a lot. I have one sister and I did not know men well. I think I may have chosen James for social reasons and I married what you might call well, and at my wedding people in the Isle of Wight were quite impressed with all the Crossleys who outnumbered them by, say, ten pews to six, and were rather better dressed and looking generally.

I had to find a Kleenex, wipe my pen, my mouth and try to get the blue stuff off my early life. Perhaps I should include the early marriage bit, explain it wasn't forced on me, i.e. I wasn't pregnant at the time. Instead I wrote of James. I quite liked this description on the whole:

At 22 James Crossley had a sort of pudgy sensuality. He was, it might be said, bon-viveurish. I liked good food as well. You couldn't get it on the Isle of Wight, although my sister has an Egon Ronay book—she lives there still, and says there are some places mentioned now.

Perhaps James Crossley came to be a little gross. But then he took up sport. Until he started off around the world he never did a thing by halves. That journey though: he stopped half way, at Katmandu, turned back. . . .

35

Monday: Noon

The sun was coming out as I set off to look for Clo. Our road is Florence Avenue by name. It is a nice straight flattish road and the tarmac on it pale and worn. The pavements are a deeper grey and over this in spring time, summer, autumn, hang the flowering trees, none very tall, for this street only came into existence forty years ago. It is my age, this street, Joel's age as well. The privet hedges round the gardens and the fences, wattle new and old, the palish tarmac all combine to give our avenue a versatile and dappled ambience.

From Florence Avenue you pass the turnings into Mavis Grove and Muriel Crescent, also Edna Close where houses are detached. The parade of shops, off-licence, corner shop and launderette are just a step away on Phyllis Road, a thoroughfare for traffic which sets the bounds of this development.

I drove down to the market square soon after noon, and circled round. A statue of King Edward VII occupies a central place and cars park round it on the cobbles. In winter, winds from all directions gust down from surrounding hills and sweep it clean. It's hardly bearable to walk across the market square cold days in winter time.

There is a café here. It's called the Café des Chevaux and has red tables, chairs and a red and white striped awning over these. Clo is often seen here with her friends from the sixth-form college just behind the square. I have to say at nineteen she is rather older than her fellow students. She tends to choose a different subject every year which means she has to start again. I'm sure, however, that she'll come out with at least one A level in the end.

She was not there and so I drove on up the hill the other

side, the southern side where houses are much bigger than on our side of the town. Here they are set back in gardens and detached. Except the house where Maurice lives which is an old stone terrace house. I stopped beside the low stone wall behind which there's a dusty laurel hedge, and pushed the gate to open it. I would have banged the gate behind me if it was not so completely rusted to its hinges. I needed to give warning of approach.

Because I once came up this garden path and, getting no reply to knocking at the door, I looked into the front room, through a big bay window where the curtains were drawn back. And there I saw a bed and on it was a naked bottom pounding up and down. I looked away. It might be Clo beneath since it seemed likely it was Maurice on the top. I would have looked away in any case, and later I discovered it was not Clo after all, but Sylvia, a friend of hers from college who had looked in for a cup of sugar from the flat above.

I never mentioned what I'd seen to Clo, but once she said: "I'm sorry about Sylvia. She doesn't have him often. It was bad luck that I have a double British Constitution Thursday mornings."

I admired her lack of jealousy. If it had been Joel and Barbara, say, I would have shot her, Barbara, dead, although I have a very good relationship with her. Or rather I'd have maimed her with whatever handy weapon I could find and wished a long and lingering death on her.

Clo gave up British Constitution, took up art. This morning, though, the curtains were across the window of the downstairs room. I knocked upon the door. The big and heavy mahogany-panelled door was slightly open and I pushed it further. There was a row of plastic bell-pushes beside it, but I knew these didn't work. Maurice is no handyman and Clo does what needs doing in the flat like cleaning, decorating, not a lot of it, but still she does it. Maurice is not practical. He may be soft and kind and seems to have a host of friends who seem to feel a magnetism which I have not savoured yet, I'm sad to say.

The door scraped on loose shreds of lino as I pushed it wide and walked inside. The hall towered over me. This house is huge and once must have housed an Edwardian family of some substance. But now, however warm the day, it felt more than a little damp. A smell of cats persisted. Someone, maybe Clo, had swept the hall. The dust was at the edges in small piles. Maurice has three rooms, the front room where he sleeps, the back room where he studies his astrology, and behind that a kitchen. I stood in the cavernous hall and called out "Clo! It's Mummy! Maurice, it's Clo's Mum!" My voice just echoed. There was emptiness.

The bedroom door was open. The pile of double mattresses which form the bed was bare. Sheets and blankets folded as if the place had been vacated. Only Clo, I thought, would fold the bedclothes up like that.

The other room: this would have been the dining-room for the large Edwardian family. There was this vast and heavy table which they used to eat upon. It's often piled with books, but these had gone to Stonehenge and to Glastonbury with him. A heavy load; they will have hitched. I saw them in my mind's eye, him and Clo with heavy rucksacks on the motorway. I wonder if her rucksack did by any chance contain his books. The rucksack with a hole, the one she lost.

Dark and empty now, this room, and dank as well, walls painted brown. Clo painted them that way because she said she wanted it to be like it had been. When that family lived here. She didn't think they would have had William Morris paper, but she thought brown walls. She'd scraped off lots of paper, found brown walls. She thought a lot about that family, gave them names as well and said the father was a tyrant and the mother fat and loving. They had a cook, a nanny and a housemaid like she'd read about in books. Not that she thought that families could be like that, not now. Not that she blamed me for not having one like that. But it was fun to think about sometimes. I thought of Clo and wished I'd brought my cardigan.

The sun-charts and the star-charts on the wall hung down at corners where the Blutack had come off. Perhaps I'd disillusioned Maurice in his work with my refusal of a horoscope for free.

A photo of him there above the marble fireplace in the sunless room. Thin face and thin moustache, bare hollow chest, sad eyes: "He's lovely and soft," said Clo in early rapture.

Another photo: Clo herself, naked but cut off above the breasts. She glows, has marvellously slanting eyes. A student-friend of theirs took these, the photos, when Clo first moved in two years back.

Perhaps I should have said to Maurice: "Yes—how kind", and put the horoscope away and never looked at it. She loves him. I love her. And did the cheerful mother of the Edwardian family throw her arms out wide to welcome into this big house the man her daughter loved?

I get spellbound by photographs. I find all photos very moving, more moving often than the presence of the person photographed. For instance, there's a picture of James he sent not long ago from Ethiopia. I had it framed and put it on the wall at home. I did it for the children's sake. It is half hidden by a fern, but there he is as he is now—or was three months ago or so—and on a mountain pass with sandals and a staff. He wears a robe of kinds, a sort of toga draped about him. And his hair is massive, fuzzy round his massive face. One gold ear-ring in an ear. The message on the back says: 'Lovely people here. Am learning Amharic'. The envelope in which the photo came bore a postmark 'Gondar'. The stamp was Ethiopian.

"I thought there was a war in Ethiopia," said Jamie.

"That wouldn't put your father off," I said.

"I thought he stood for peace and loving kindness like Joel does."

"That may have been a passing phase," I said, "for after all your father—way back—did enjoy his National Service."

"But Joel now says he's glad he did his army training . . ."

"Well, luckily Joel had a fairly peaceful time . . . the rudiments of self-defence I'm sure he understands . . ."

I left the house where Maurice lives. The building echoed as I closed the door. I wrote a note and pinned it to the mantelpiece beneath their photographs: 'Come home when you get back, Love M.' (for Monica or Mummy) and drove home slowly through the town now busy, lunchtime shoppers strolling, sitting in the sun.

And went into our house and found another card from Clo which came by second post:

That Keith, amazing bloke already mentioned, has invited us to join him at his seaside home. I think we might just go. M. rather low needs a rest.

No kisses at the bottom, but the card was posted Thursday last. I puzzled that she'd said that Maurice needed rest. He is a very restful person I'd have thought, unlikely to exhaust himself.

A little breeze through open window ruffled ferns and James in Ethiopia appeared, was covered up again. He comes home once a year or so since turning back at Katmandu. He stares around this house which is not his but which is full of things which once were his. He wears a suit I'd helped him choose twelve years ago. I have to try hard to remember if he has sugar in his tea or coffee.

Monday: p.m.

By second post as well—a letter from Joel's Mum:

Dear Joel and Monica,
    So pleased to hear that all is well with you. It is quite well with me as well. I won at Bingo Tuesday last and didn't do so badly on Gold Cup day either. But Mr Cookson lost out badly on the 4.15, and so we didn't have our usual binge.
    Am glad to hear your children, Monica, are doing well. I like to think of kiddies in the summer. And did I thank you in my last for Joel's new book of poems? I thought they were quite nice. Must close. Your loving Mum.

Joel hardly ever goes to see his mother now. Because she lives in Blackpool, what she likes to do is walk along the front, play Bingo and the fruit machines. So I go to see her on my own because, although I don't like Bingo much, I do enjoy the fruit machines. Last time I went Joel's Mum and I got jackpots, both of us, and put our winnings on a Derby winner.
    Joel's Mum is happy on the whole, living as she does with Mr Cookson. She doesn't mind not seeing Joel, she says. She is quite fond of him but gets confused with all the things he's done. She likes a man to be a thing and stay that way, and doesn't understand that all the things Joel's been have been but as a search for something like a true vocation. For instance Mr Cookson she can introduce to friends as having been on railways all his life. And Joel loves her, I think, and doesn't grudge a penny of the money that he sends her every now and then, except he fears it goes into the tills of multi-million leisure empires.
    That book of poems—*Two in One*—referred to in the

41

letter from Joel's Mum—is dedicated to me, and in the one review he had—the *Bingley Telegraph and Argus*—we were pleased to read:

> A touching piece. Joel Trotter must be one of the more positively loving of the group of Yorkshire poets now approaching middle age.

Which is quite true. But otherwise we are anonymous, unsung, unmentioned in the local papers unless our group 'New Pathways' has a major poet reading. Though Pru got nation-wide reviews for *Counterpunch*, the rest of us (even Gerry) accept our role and do not envy those who make the headlines. On the whole that is.

On rare occasions Joel gets angry that his work is unacknowledged. Of all of us I have to say he has most promise, taking words and thought beyond the normal and expected bounds of possibility. You think you know what poetry is and then you hear a poem that he's written, which is so completely new and different that you know you never knew at all what poetry was.

Not only does Joel stick to form, but searches for new forms. But never breaks the old. Sometimes he rants around the rush mats in our long extended room and throws his arms about and narrowly misses plants. "Why," he sometimes cries in desperation, "why the villanelle, the sonnet, both Petrarchan and the other, the quatrain, the Spenserian stanza? Why not the Joel? The Trotter?" We do not try to calm him because it is this kind of anger which inspires him most to work.

He flings himself outside, banging the glazed garden door and nearly falling into the courgettes, shaking heads of sweet-corn outside and of ferns inside. I shout: "I want you to be famous, darling, all the same. We all want you to be as famous as you want to be." And then, in spite of being fairly used to scenes like that, I tend to shake a little. Bruce is comforting on these occasions. He hovers, makes me cups of tea and sits with me to play a soothing game of Scrabble, finds my glasses—and my valium should I have need of it.

Joel always comes back full of humility and apologies. He's probably run down the recreation field and back, and comes in calm. He throws himself with head upon my knees and says how could he have expressed such anger when it makes me shake and puts me off my work, which is in its way quite important too. And either joins in with the game or goes out to the workshop for some planing or a bit of tongue and groove, and comes in with another bookshelf or another bedside table.

But that is not the view of Joel I want to give. I rather think of him in terms of Horace, Book Three, Ode Three, which begins:

A just man, steady of intention
Who remains unshaken by the clamour . . .

He did appreciate the *Telegraph and Argus* review. But now he needs another little triumph. As Pru so often says, a man's libido suffers without public praise: "And I should know," she adds with bitterness, but Joel was not himself last night and even though he listened while I spoke of doubts about our sending Jamie off, he left this morning on his little Honda motor-cycle, drawn of face and saying nothing else.

This evening when he came to fetch me at the launderette, he stood outside and waited till I'd finished. I watched the clothes inside the tumbler-drier flick and fly in space around the drum while Joel was pacing on the pavement with his hands behind his back.

I sat and mused on random shapes the drier makes with clothes. The launderette is on the corner at the end of Phyllis Road. It has a plane tree just outside, a litter bin against the tree. Not far away the fish and chip shop, and the litter that collects from this gets scattered round about. Joel bent and picked some bits of greasy paper up and carried them and put them in the bin and then resumed his pacing, chin in air, beard jutting at the grey and almost wintry sky. A woman who had clothes inside a washer said: "He doesn't like to come in here, your hubby then?"

I said: "He's very sensitive to atmosphere. There's too much plastic, metal and unusual smells in here."

"You what?" she said.

"He is a poet," I explained.

He went on walking up and down. He put his hand into his pocket and he took a notebook out, consulted it and went on pacing with his hands behind his back, unconscious of the woman staring at him. "He looks right quiet," she said. "At least he's quiet," she said again, as if to tell me that her husband was not quiet, but noisy and annoying to her in some way.

She sat and watched her clothes within the circle of the window of the washer, and back to back with her, I watched mine in the drier, watched how one of Joel's black socks soared up and wrapped itself around a pair of Bruce's purple underpants. Then Bruce's T-shirt with AHOY THERE SAILOR written on it, flew up and took off with my flouncy skirt.

The woman said, "He's thinking up a poem, then?"

"He might be, or a moral point."

"He looks more like a vicar when you look at him," she said.

"He ought to be a person of authority," I said.

He hates the seedy nature of such places as this launderette where people sit with empty eyes or smoke and use some dingy ashtray piled with old fag ends. Compassionate as well, he's tortured with the contradictions that the launderette suggests, relieving as it does to some extent the burden of a woman's life, while lowering her sense of taste. I looked outside. It seemed the mist had now returned or was it just the condensation on the windows of the launderette? He grabbed my arm as I came out and looked at me as if to search me for contamination: "I hate that lousy place for you," he said.

But later he was standing by the sweetcorn and I saw a gentle giant like on the tins on supermarket shelves. He does deserve more out of life. I think the Horace Ode I quoted here to illustrate the steadfast quality of Joel was actually

44

about Augustus. Never mind. Pru once said that we need in a second marriage to extol our partners higher than we did the first time round, to justify the act. She does it all the time she says—a lie. I say I do not do it out of need. I do it since it is deserved and true.

His notebook in the car—he had been shaping up another Horace Ode. Book Three, Ode Six: 'Fecunda culpae saecula nuptias':

A generation this in evil rich
Has stained the home, the marriage bond and which
Has fouled pure springs of blood
And sent down ruin in the river's flood.

A funny light, a yellowness behind the mist. He drove me home in silence and I thought: perhaps he needs the yin of fighting *and* the yang of peace. He should command the hordes as they sweep down upon the cohorts of the giant monopolies. Such problems as Clo, Gerry's mid-life crisis, Jamie's softly falling tears would fade into insignificance if Joel was out at war.

Oh race and nation, people, city!
Your daughters dance in all unchastity
And bend to learn the Greekish whim
In every artful and provoking limb.

"That's very good," I said, "but what about the sons?"

Of Bruce, it could not well be said he's self-contained. He's gained a lot from breaking with Theresa for a time, I guess, and in his friendly way has spread himself around the local girls. He's not been short of what he quaintly calls his Harry leg-over. And Joel, I have to say, encourages, and listens father-like to Harry-conquest stories. And I myself am not complaining since it lends a lightness to our household on the whole.

Tonight however there was nothing of that kind. We ate our pizza made of wholemeal flour, our new potatoes and our salad with some mild French dressing on, and Joel seemed

45

quiet again, until Bruce said, endearingly, "This is quite a bonza Peter pizza, isn't it?"

At last Joel responded with light remark, a kind of joke which is to do with Bruce's auntie back in Parramatta. Bruce's auntie used to say to him when he was little: "Get your happy pants on, Bruce." Joel often uses this and says to Bruce "O.K. Bruce? happy pants?" It makes them laugh. I join in sometimes saying, "No more grouchy pants, then Bruce?" although he very seldom gets in moods like Joel. In fact he helps our ups and downs, confusions with our mutuality, all that sort of thing. He pleases Joel—there is a readiness about Bruce. Joel sees himself as patron to a future film director in a way.

We ate and briefly laughed. The sun had now come out again and lit on tops of sweetcorn and of sunflower heads. A glow spread right across the recreation field. The grey had melted back into the sky which now was deep intensive blue. We'd joked a bit but silence fell again. I felt resentment coming out of Joel because I'd challenged him when coming home. And Bruce had given up his efforts to dispel the gloom and sat there looking distant, pale blue eyes beneath his fringe of soft blond hair. Some laughter from the recreation field enhanced the sense of stifled life within the room. And so I said because I couldn't think what else to say: "I spoke to someone at the launderette."

Then Joel put down his knife and fork and stared out straight across the garden at the hedge, the field, the distant trees beyond the field as if to say is this the level of our wit, the way we speak about our apprehension of the world? Is this the raconteuse I've married, the kind of intellectual chat we must expect because our lives are now so low in major content? At least that's what he seemed to say; that was the undercurrent or the subtext of his gesture—laying down his knife and fork. The words he spoke however were: "I think I've had enough of pizza on the whole."

I turned my head away. I may have blinked back tears. I also looked outside, but not so far. The grass upon our lawn in this late sun had turned electric green where lit against our eastern boundary fence.

The pizza was a good one too, a mushroom and green pepper one, with anchovies. Perhaps Bruce sensed the rising air of tension, twigged this cloud which seemed to hover, threatening and pregnant round the plates and glasses, emanating mostly so it seemed out of the deep green glazed salad bowl which a potter friend had made us as a wedding gift. At any rate Bruce said: "Well, have you any news of Clo?"

"I told you, didn't I?" I said, "she lost her rucksack just the other day?" and turned back to the window once again.

Joel said: "No more to lose I'd say."

"How do you mean, my love?" and with a sense of panic rising in my breast because he didn't answer that, I said: "If you mean what I think you mean, that isn't very kind."

"My darling heart, you rise too quickly to my little crack."

I took the plates and piled them on the sink and turned the tap to watch the steamy water splash around the stainless steel and bounce against the crockery. Back at the table from one corner of my eye, I saw Joel look at Bruce and Bruce at Joel. They were exchanging glances. I was now apart from them, a figure of some fun, a scolding mother.

"Come on now," said Joel. "Who has got grouchy pants on now?"

I had to stay beside the sink for several minutes in order to compose my features and I washed the dishes very well instead of leaving them to Bruce as usual.

The sun stayed out, but something had been fractured in such bonhomie as there had been. The two men switched the television on and watched some girls on 'It's a Knockout' slipping down in blue-ish water with their T-shirts tight and wet, and Joel and Bruce both cheered.

There is a sense in which I am consoled by Bruce's interest shared with Joel in legs and breasts and hips. At least it does ensure their friendship does not ripen into homosexuality. I could feel most excluded if it did.

47

I went outside and mused upon the irreducibilities of life and waited till the sun went off the plants and then got out the watering-can.

In Phyllis Road you find the pub, the Lamb and Flag, our local, where we go each Monday night and sometimes several other nights as well. And there tonight were many of our friends including Gerry, Pru and Ron and Barbara, also Malcolm who has recently become a window cleaner and Pete, the steel erector, many more as well. We seem to have a warm relationship with all these people.

I walked a little on my own, let Bruce and Joel stride on ahead. I sniffed the evening air and felt revived enough to notice details like the television aerials etched sharply on the steel of evening blue, which might just be a poem if I put my mind to it. A haiku is a shortish form and one of these has come since then:

A northern twilight
Television aerials
Signalling to me.

But here's the Lamb and Flag inside, the 'thirties decor, bulbous, early Odeon-like and comfortable. A long and solid bar to lean against. I think I listened for some time to Ron regaling me with anecdotes about the lady on the other side of town who wants her bathroom black and gold with real brass taps, a sunken bath.

And Pru was chatting up a man in double-glazing, not about the insulation of her house, but on the subject of her home-town, Leicester, where he comes from too. She likes to get things right, does Pru. The novel that she's working on is set in Leicester and she has not been down there for several years. He was describing for her the one-way traffic system there and what the new pedestrian precinct is like.

And Gerry just along the bar was treating several people to his stories of the time he read with Basil Bunting and the time he caught a glimpse of Philip Larkin on a train. And then he started on the yarn about the lady poet whom he could have had when reading at a Festival in Wetherby (or rather after reading at a Festival in Wetherby), and one about his first wife and an ironing board, the point of which I've never fathomed quite.

And Joel, competing, bless his heart (for drink had mellowed me) came in with one about a girl in Portsmouth, which has a different punchline every time he tells it. I often wonder what the truth about the Portsmouth story was. Joel's factual but embroidered fictions are very chauvinist, but all the same a joy to listen to. One of the boys I am—when at the pub I sometimes think. I thought of this while Ron was telling me about the new biography he's got which is about Lord Halifax and quite explains the causes of the Second World War.

Then people seemed to move away from Gerry, and Joel began to talk to someone else who's in the business of recycling bottle glass. I would have joined him, talked with him and reasserted solidarity, but by that time I was involved with Gerry who was being rather hostile. Which he gets when people haven't stayed to listen to his stories at the Lamb and Flag.

Not far from us was Pru, whose eyes were lighting up. Presumably she'd made the great connection that a double-glazing man might be exactly right as chief protagonist in *See-Through Man.* She loves coincidences like that and thinks they must portend well for her work in hand.

But Gerry stood beside me saying, "Ah what boots it?" several times.

"What boots what, Gerry?" I said, moving slightly nearer Ron.

"Ah you! Ah, ha, the lovely Monica. So quiet, reflective, pondering and pure!"

This was a new tack from the troubled mind. He went on, leaning on the bar: "The one who follows but who hardly speaks, the feminist who listens and bites later only to her fellow feminists . . . so pure!" he said again.

I looked at Pru who had sat down and let the double-glazing man put one arm round her. "I thought that it was you who had become the pure," I said to Gerry.

He bought himself another gin and tonic and, to be quite fair to him, he got me a Campari too, but then he said: "And where's the lovely Clo? Not practising the purity, I guess?"

I snapped at him; "And how were you in lust when young, my friend? And have I not been hearing boasts of prowess in that field tonight?"

The pub was at its fullest now, just half an hour to closing time, and Gerry had to raise his voice to say: "Ah! Fists unbound, we fight with tooth and claw."

"That is what nature's red in, Gerry. At least use your quotations right."

Ron, slow sometimes to understand the nuance of an argument, came in with, "Tell you what our Monica! Your Clo, she hasn't had our Ashley yet."

"There has to be a precedent," said Gerry and I kicked him in the shins. "Why don't you go and join the Festival of Light," I said, "and fuck your way round that? And come back with the stories of your conquests which will entertain us all?"

Perhaps I went too far. I never speak like that to anyone apart from Gerry, for many reasons which I'll try to sort out in due course. So crowded was the pub Joel did not hear the rumpus in the corner. I would have thrown the rest of my Campari over Gerry had there been enough to throw. I pushed my way between the mass of bodies, pushed the swing-door open and I went into the car park where there is, surrounding it, a chain-link fence. I needed to sit down, but could not sit on that, the fence. I leaned upon the bonnet of a car.

I heard them coming after me. I heard Ron saying: "By, but I've never heard her blaze like that. You did wrong, Gerry lad. She's worried about her kiddies like. It isn't any fault of hers the way they have turned out. You get good genes and bad genes and I'll say this for her Jamie, he . . ."

"No Ron," I shouted out across the car park and I banged my fist on what turned out to be Gerry's vintage Lanchester. "No, Ron, it isn't genes, it's life. It can be all explained by life but not excused."

Then Barbara was beside me too and telling me I had no call to shout at Ron like that. And somewhere Pru was saying that I seemed to think I had immunity from criticism because I pleaded motherhood as an excuse.

"That isn't fair," I said. "I haven't mentioned my kids once all night."

"The emptiness of all existence, what a load of rubbish," Barbara said. "Pre-menstrual tension if you ask me . . ." and Pru was telling Barbara that she was a traitor to her sex. I left them, started home. I almost ran. Another haiku came:

Night sky unsmiling
When sunrays warmed our rooftop,
Then you cared.

The last line is two syllables short, but never mind. I'm in disgrace. And Joel so full of concern for what occurred, although he took no part in it because he had not heard it going on, sits there at desk with head in hands and cannot work. It won't have done a lot for his libido either.

I speak to Gerry metaphorically. I take him back ten years. "You said with such conviction that life had no limits. You even wrote a poem called *Man's Reach Is What It's All About.* You acted as you preached. The day you jumped a five-barred gate and said: 'Let's have a Festival of Anarchy at Kirkby Overblow.' On May Day too."

And then I look at Joel and think: 'And you believed him too, with all your brains, in spite of being the just man steady of intention who is unshaken by the clamour, you used to swing on metaphoric chandeliers with Gerry. Now you sit like Rodin's Penseur weeping for the city and the youth.'

I want to say to both of them: "You said send up balloons with LOVE and JOY on them. You sent me to the shop to order them. You sent me off for fireworks out of season all the way

51

to Halifax or was it Huddersfield? You said we'd all wear T-shirts with a poem printed on. Who got them printed then? You wrote a poem about bicycles and got us riding up and down in Roundhay Park in Leeds, and when you had a puncture, who went off to buy the puncture-mending outfit on a Sunday? And no one would have been there on your May Day Festival if I had not put up the notices. And when it snowed but few of us were there to have our anarchy in a pub in Kirkby Overblow.

The balloons took off, but many blew across the road. In May I needed gloves and muddled up the strings. Balloons, still knotted, blew across the road and burst on railings on the other side. A pink one did escape and rise, blown west between two trees against a steely sky, which gave us all at least one poem.

The world was shifting on its axis as you thought, and we would help it in the transmutations that resulted from that shift but now you scream at what has followed on.

But Joel would say that we were adults then, albeit in our second adolescence. I look at him and want to say: "I followed you with shortened skirt, with shiny boots and came straight from the tennis club and rugby dance, James Crossley being at the zenith of his sporting phase."

Tuesday: a.m.

The newest shop in town, a supermarket. The car park sparkled in the morning sun, kaleidoscope of colours. Cars this year have come in fruity and flamboyant shades of emerald and flame, electric blue and buttercup. And rows and rows of them, bristling with aerials and chromium which catches bouncing sunlight, shimmers, coruscates. The blue in the sky had lost its steely edge and come up smiling, and a little wind, a south one at a guess because it ruffled you a bit. Barbara in Lotus with dark glasses on and brown arms in her Jaeger sleeveless, hair highlit like the morning, sweeping round to find a parking space. The long low car was nosing round, me sitting in the front.

A high point in the town, a view of hills and country to the north with tills which ring along the barnlike space which thrums with music and the clank of wheels and metal spokes. I waited there for Barbara with my metal basket in my hand beside the deep-freeze counter. Oh, wicked richness of the place, past which Joel hurries head-down if he walks downtown with me, ignoring also as he must the Bingo Hall (heads down three times a day) and headscarfed women waiting to go in. And yet for one born and brought up in Blackpool, he must have been aware of things like this when young, when in his pram maybe. Although the rumour is his mother was so poor they didn't have a pram. I see her now with Joel in shawl strapped to her and a paper bag with shopping in her other hand, lights flashing from arcades into his tiny eyes, the smell of pickled onions, candy floss and fish and chips.

While I was growing up along a country lane down south, and horse and cow manure were probably the only offensive

53

smells. My mother had to pull the straying brambles from the wheelspokes of my coachbuilt pram.

Good news today, for Barbara that is. At least she thinks it is good news. For young Lorraine, who works at Boots, has taken Ashley's diamond ring and is engaged to him. I dare not say I think they are too young, for she and I are friends again, the harsh words which she spoke to me last night officially forgotten by today. And more good news: her Nicola has rung to say there is a bad new tear in their balloon; they may not race at all. And Barbara, blooming, threw all caution to the winds (unlike the Cambridge University Balloon Society) and aimed to fill at least one shopping trolley to the brim with good rich goods.

But no good news for me. Our courgette plants, all but three, had withered in the night. Their stalks went brown, collapsed, gave out. And then a card from Jamie came: 'A.N.O.K. and food disgusting. Have lost pen.' The card was done in pencil. There were several kisses at the bottom and some splodges which might just be tears. The picture was of rain on Windermere.

Watch Barbara coming down towards me with her trolley loaded up and piled with illustrated tins of frozen orange juice and big red packs of sirloin steak and fillet steak and envelopes of coral pink smoked salmon for Ron's lunchtime sandwiches. She paused to pick from here a tub of double cream, from there a pound of fluted English butter.

While I sauntered by the deep-freeze counter, not to buy from there, but only to observe the ornamental fulsomeness of illustrations on the cheesecake boxes and the packets of eclairs, the swirls of whipped cream, dabs of wine-dark fruity juice. Then moved to where things more savoury, less luscious, were presented. I stood while people paused and plunged their hands down into icy depths and took up cases of two dozen vol-au-vent or cheese-and-onion pies or chef-style stroganoff and piled them in their trolleys, then wheeled on.

I had my pound of porridge oats—request from Joel I'd welcomed since he had just murmured as he left the house and turned down egg and bacon with disgust, that porridge was a thing which just might make him feel that life was worth the living once again. Oh, how he balks me in my wish to serve good food to him! Perhaps it is that Joel only has to see a meal laid out with nice contrasting colours so it looks like an advertisement, for him to be switched off food completely.

A figure moving in one corner of my vision, coming up along the baking aids with loping heavy step. The contents of the basket in his hand were, like mine, few, although I did not notice in great detail: perhaps a half a pound of margarine, a tin of baked beans and a loaf of sliced white bread. A tallish stooping form, a narrow drooping man.

I froze beside the deep-freeze counter at that moment, shivered just a little, stood stock still and did not move my head to look around. Perhaps the brilliance of the day outside had got to me, when flashing sun on bumpers blinded me. Perhaps a foretaste of my own mid-life crisis is the onset of confusion of one object with another. Perhaps I was unfair to Gerry and there is a natural order where like here more women always will push trolleys while the men stand masterful and bored beside their speedy Scimitars and Opels and boast of conquests which they'd scoff at scornfully if women made. Perhaps courgettes are dying in our garden since, although I water every night, I have excluded them in absent-mindedness.

The figure came up on my right with slow but steady stride and passed me and was then seen on my left. It's said that ornithologists first recognise a bird by flight and not by plumage. This figure's face I could not see, but from the movement it was Maurice. There was the khaki jacket and the hair which hangs like spaniels' ears. The jacket, short of sleeves which made the wrists jut out, large hands. Nor did I turn my head to ratify. Nor did he, if it was he, stop and speak. And Barbara, trolley high and overflowing, processed towards me now, majestically.

And was Ron wrong to think that genes cause all, right

55

from the start, and was I wrong and Jamie will be James all over, take up sport when he is thirty-five, at forty give that up and go around the world half way? And Clo will marry soon, divorce, remarry, then, when standing in a supermarket in the 1990s wonder where on earth she is.

That car park slopes a bit. The trolley was a wayward one and Barbara needed me to help her steer it, leaning back against its weight each side. We piled the cartons and the fruit directly in the Lotus boot. I bent to run and catch a rolling melon as it took the slope, and caught instead a glimpse of Maurice standing there against the sun some hundred yards away.

He'd gone though, when we drove out of the entrance. Not a sign of him. I held the melon in my lap and talked to Barbara of the price of coffee, whether Kenyan blend was better than American and what the buffet meal would be on Friday at their Silver Wedding party.

Our house was empty, but it struck me as a haunted house. A breeze had got up blowing curtains. There was ringing in my ears but not the telephone. In Clo's room there are Hindu bells which have the same tone as the telephone and these were moving by the open window, which I shut.

She plays loud music, Barbara does, like Demis Roussos, Neil Sedaka, Frank Sinatra. I went on with my early life with James, about the time we went to dinner with some people and I neither sparkled nor was gay. James said, excusing me, that I was quite artistic in a way and had these moods: "What art," they said, "does she pursue?"

"She is a poet," James said, maybe just because he couldn't think what else to say. And so I said: "All right, I'll be a poet then." I carried in my head the thought that poets didn't have to be too nice to people on the whole. I mean I know you do have to be nice to people, but it isn't very easy on the whole, and poets were the legislators of the world I thought I'd read, and luckily for me a lot of people liked my early poems, which were angry in a way and with a sense of protest which I did not know was in me to express.

56

And James was quite surprised as well, and that was when he said: "I think I'll go around the world," which was a good idea because he didn't need the money from his job. He was a rich man now, some Crossley money having come his way, inherited. Now he could wear an ear-ring, grow his hair which he had wanted to for years.

I somehow didn't feel it should be quite so easy for a man to up and leave his family, so I said: "But *can* you go?"

He said: "Your father travelled all his life."

"But that was only in between Southampton and either Cherbourg or Le Havre . . ."

"He did it for his whole career. That would add up to going round the world," said James. He made some calculations mileagewise which proved his point. I did some too, which did not prove the point. We did not argue much about his going, but we argued out the mileage endlessly.

About that time I fell in love with Joel. I trembled, shook around the knees, clouds opened, angels puffed their cheeks and blew their trumpets in the sky. I knew not what I did, it could be said . . . I paused here, thought a bit, then wrote: 'I knew exactly what I did, I think.'

I heard the postman coming up the road, exchanging chat with people as he came. I saw him turn into our path and heard the letter fall on to the mat and went downstairs:

Clo's writing slopes, is rounded, large and somehow the address took up the surface of the envelope. Addressed to all of us it was, to 'Mrs M Trotter (Mummy), Mr J Trotter (Big Daddy), Master J Crossley (little master) and Mr Bruce (a lusty Aussie comic) Carter', from all of which I sensed that Clo was in a happy mood, on song again.

Wy Worry,
The Lizard,
Cornwall.

Dear all, I know this sounds a silly place, but it really is called that. Keith and Nina think some loony man from Manchester (they're all retired from Manchester down

57

here) had lost his fortune probably and thought 'Oh sod it' when he bought this place. It's teeny weeny and it's thatched. It's in a hollow and the gales blow over it. But they have to put some special gungey stuff upon the roof each autumn just in case they don't—blow over it—the gales I mean. I am O.K.

I really am. I hope to get things in perspective soon. It wasn't Keith who brought things to a head. He helped. He helped to get me out of it. And as to Maurice—I don't know. I hope that Jamie is O.K. at camp and Bruce as well (but not at camp etcetera) and kisses everyone.

Your Clo.

There was a postscript.

Keith and Nina are the couple I am staying with and they have twins. As you will gather Maurice has not come. It may be for the best. The sea is kind of turquoise here.

So that explained the Maurice sighting in the supermarket. I wrote to Clo at once and told her all the news, as many things that I could think of that she'd like to hear. I sat there in the garden under sky now sapphire blue and flecked with high up clouds and said I'd heard from Jamie: he was well, and Bruce was well and Joel was fairly well and Pru and Gerry were a little tense about the Grassington Award. I wrote and said that we were cheerful on the whole and that we'd bought a garden frame, or rather ordered one, and then I chewed my pen and said that maybe it was better that she'd broken up with Maurice, but I added sorry and all that. Then picked her letter up again and realised that she had not said they'd broken up, but only that he wasn't there.

So tore my letter up and sent a telegram instead. Because the thing she didn't know, the most important news perhaps was that she had to go to Perpignan and that her father was about to be . . .

CLO CROSSLEY C/O KEITH WY WORRY LIZARD CORNWALL STOP PLEASE RING HOME URGENT STOP.

Then I changed the last part to 'PLEASE RING HOME FAIRLY URGENT STOP' in case she thought that something untoward had happened, and I sat and listened to the sound of singing and felt like dancing since I'd heard from Clo.

Tuesday: p.m.

The day was warm, the sky still sapphire blue. I felt a poem coming on about the sky and rushed upstairs to check in my thesaurus other kinds of blue. Cerulean perhaps. A cloudless feeling though there were high clouds. A sense of more to come. An azure sky? A sense of trust in Clo, a vision of her toes in sea with twin in either hand in turquoise sea, and in the garden once again I took the dead courgette plants, threw them on our compost heap and bent and studied the remaining three alive to see if they could be by any chance cross-pollinated.

"He's come back on his own," a girl who'd just arrived was saying as she sat there on the lawn.

"Who's come back on his own?" I turned and looked at her. A girl I think I know, a friend of Clo's. A girl who thought I knew her anyway.

"Why Maurice! He has come back on his own."

"Oh yes, I know . . ."

"Came back last night . . ."

"I see." I'd fetched our garden book by then and checked up on courgettes. It seems a female flower has swellings at the base. I fetched my glasses, knelt down peering close at them. The three remaining plants were female all of them.

"I spent the night with him . . ."

"Oh did you now?"

The girl was small with curly hair. Her hair was nice. I wondered if she'd had a perm. She smoked a cigarette with jerky movements of her hands and head as if she wasn't used to smoking much. Of course! This was the girl upstairs from Maurice who had been under him the day I went there unexpectedly. So that was it!

"Well, not like that," she said. "I mean he's very . . . down."

"Poor Maurice . . ." I was looking at the tiny swellings on the courgette flowers and peering down into their yellow funnels checking stamens wondering if there was someone who had male courgettes I could collect the pollen from.

"Oh yes!" she said.

"Yes what?"

"I mean he does want Clo. I mean he wants her back. I mean . . ."

"I don't see what that has to do with us. I mean if *you* want him . . ."

"I only stayed to keep him company . . ."

"How kind of you . . ."

"He keeps on taking overdoses . . ."

"For goodness sake," I said, and down in one of those courgettes I saw some dust which clung to stamens . . .

"Ten sleeping pills," she said. She bit her finger. She looked younger just a bit than Clo. Still kneeling down I craned my neck to look at her. It seemed amazing that she'd coped with Maurice all last night if he was taking overdoses.

"But he'd be dead," I said, "I don't believe it honestly. He couldn't have."

"He could and did . . . he sort of walked around and chucked them in his mouth and looked at me and said that Clo had finished with him. Just like that. He said she'd gone off with this other bloke and left him in the middle of the night. Not took the tent, he said."

"It *is* our tent," I said. "He may be taking vitamins and fooling you."

"Oh, well I dunno that. At any rate I heard him there and haven't been up since. I mean to my flat." She looked a little cold, this girl and hugged her knees. She wore a cotton jacket and looked pale as if she hadn't seen the sun for days.

"Well he was walking round, despairing like."

"I saw him in the supermarket shopping, dear."

"I know. He did go there, but he is sort of desperate . . .

He says he thinks that Clo has gone to Cornwall or some place."

"She has."

"He said for me to ask you her address . . ."

"I'm sure that Clo will get in touch with him when she is ready to . . ."

"He's going on at me."

"Why don't you go home to your Mum and get out of his way?"

"My Mum's in Newcastle."

By this time I was quite convinced that one of our courgettes had pollinated. Some dust had blown from who knows where and we would have at least one fruit-bearing plant this year. I stood up, looked down at the girl. She threw a fag end in the air. It landed on the compost heap.

"You tell him that he needs a doctor . . ."

"Yes."

"I'd like to help . . ."

She looked up. What a strange small face, I thought.

"Well then . . .?" she said.

"You tell him see a doctor . . . or psychiatrist. I think he has depended rather much on Clo," I said. "They do . . ." I wiped my spectacles with one small corner of my skirt and checked again in order to confirm the presence of the yellow dust.

"Who do?" she said.

"Men do," I said, "rely on girls too much . . ."

"Oh yeah." She hadn't thought of that it seemed.

The funnel of this yellow flower; I held it gently, looking down into that very delicate construction.

"I couldn't stand another night like that," she said. "His other friends came round, then went. He threatens like, they seem to think . . ." she flicked some ash and let it lie upon the grass and brushed it with her hand. I let that one courgette flower bounce back and then I peered into another one. This had no dust, but otherwise had swelling, embryonic fruit, as similar in every detail as the other two. "He should try ringing the Samaritans," I said.

"He won't do that."

"You tell him that I said he should . . ."

She rubbed more ash into the grass. "I'll try."

I like to get my logic right. This time I did, I think: "Either he is threatening or he is serious. If he is threatening, then no one need worry. If he is serious, then he will go to the Samaritans—or rather ring them up."

"He's done it all before," she said, "not rung them up but done things other times like this." She stood beside me. I am smallish as I mentioned in my early life, but she was tiny, barely coming to my shoulder. And yet old. Her shoulders bent she went off down the Avenue at three o'clock. I shut the door behind her feeling cold and huddled on the couch. My feet were bare. I put them under me to warm them up.

"How many times," I'd asked her when she said that he had done it all before.

"Oh lots. But you know, Clo was there. I mean the times she took him into casualty."

"She what?" I said.

"I mean the time he cut his wrists and all those times . . ."

"Oh yes," I nodded, "yes."

"You knew about those times?" She did not guess I did not know, but went off through the house and down the street. I huddled on the couch and thought how Clo had never told me, thought of all the things Clo never talked about. Though something dim and half-remembered back in May or was it April? Something about Maurice ill or having had an accident, something that she mentioned at that time. And the time he rang up in the middle of the night. "He has a nightmare. I must go," she said. "He dreams in awful oranges and flames and khaki monsters come at him," and went off on her bicycle in total dark.

Outside I fetched the rug. The clouds had joined across the sky. The sapphire, azure or cerulean had gone. And turquoise too. I wrapped the rug around me like a shawl, as what

63

seemed to be a layer of cold air blew in across the gardens to the east of us. With one bare foot I scuffed the grass, the little pile of ash left by the girl, and with one hand I bent and picked her second fag end up and threw it on the compost heap. The yellow flowers I'd looked into with deep concern were fluttering a bit. The pollen might have blown away again.

Then Pru rang up: "It is about the novel."

"Yes?"

"The lover's going to be a double-glazing man."

"I'm not surprised."

"I think I've cracked that part of it, but now I've got to get them into bed, the woman and the double-glazing man, that is. I've written her a hang-up that she has about her matrimonial bed . . ."

"That didn't worry you before. Well not in *Counterpunch* at any rate."

"The heroine of *Counterpunch* was childless though, until the childbirth at the end at any rate. This one has quite a few—I'm not sure yet how many kids. The basic thing is that I've got to have her have him in the conservatory, for reasons of the leit-motif . . . the glass you see . . . but make it stick that her motive is an inhibition at the use of her matrimonial bed . . ."

"Uh uh?" I said.

"Well, do you think that's likely on the whole?"

"I'm mixed up, Pru. I'll talk again. I'll think."

Wednesday a.m.

Last night I got Joel to put on the Caribbean shirt his mother bought him when she went with Mr Cookson to Bermuda on a package with St Leger winnings. Also his denim cap, and this he has not worn for years. He looked, you could say, almost debonair: "Quite like old times," I said, not guessing just how like old times it would turn out to be.

He said: "But you and Gerry aren't on speaking terms. We'll have to make excuses dearest heart . . ."

"That's neither here nor there," I said. "We are committed socially. I may not make much contribution to the sum of moral thought, but there are certain little rules I feel obliged to stick to or I lose my self-respect."

It was a bit like driving Jamie off to camp. I had to say to Joel: "I'm sure you'll like it once you're there." And I was right. Joel did enjoy it in the end. In fact you might say he enjoyed it like there was no tomorrow. He often thinks there's no tomorrow anyway, but in another sense.

Our host was somebody we hardly know, or hardly knew before we went. Mr Savory—Derek I must call him now since we have been so intimate—happens to be my dentist. I had some fairly complex dental work done recently, which led me to spend many hours with Mr Savory, with Derek rather, in his chair. Exchanging chat I casually revealed my contacts with the poetry world, and he at once confided me his interest in this matter. That is not unusual, mind you. Nearly every time I mention poetry, the person to whom I mention it is like to volunteer that he or she writes poetry too. This is a strange phenomenon both Joel and I have often spoken of. It tends to make us feel a little less exclusive on the whole.

65

Joel said: "We'll have to listen to his stuff all night."

I said: "I think it's really that he is a fan of Gerry's early work."

"My God," said Joel. "What have you got us into now?"

"It's all right, darling heart, I'm sure he will have heard of you as well. I only mentioned poetry once. He took me up on it." I wished that I had stuck to weather and the ring road which is being planned. This Derek is a clinically pure and fairly cuddly man with dew-sweet breath, but all the same I wish I'd stuck to being just his patient, in a way.

Joel said: "We'll come home early, O.K., sweetest love?"

"O.K."

Surprising really that this dentist who, like other dentists, is extremely rich and who I would have thought had all he needed in this life, expressed the wish for more from us. When first he'd said he'd heard of Gerry and would like to meet him, I suggested that he joined New Pathways Poetry Group ("Meets every other Wednesday, half past seven upstairs in the town hall and after in the Lamb and Flag," I said). But no, he'd rather meet the McLeHoses privately. Then Mrs Savory, Doreen, rang recently and asked us all to dinner. She had read Pru's novel *Counterpunch* and was enchanted at the idea that she'd have a chance to chat to Pru herself.

Joel said when going there: "I don't feel awfully well. I think it is my teeth."

"Oh, very funny! Ho ho ho!" I said. I was quite crisp. It must have been the extra dose of lemovite I'd taken early evening.

There was a calm about the large converted house up in the Dales that put me at my ease. Although Pru eyed the conventional but expensive furnishings with some disparagement and winked at me from time to time, I felt there was a solid structure to the place and people. Something *Daily Telegraph* about the home, the children's ponies in the field, the *Yachting Monthly* and the *Horse and Hound*, the golf clubs in the hall, the uninspiring curtains, carpets . . . although the archery equipment, snorkel tubes and climbing boots all led me to believe that Derek and Doreen must be in search of something extra in their lives.

And Doreen, hearing Joel was skilled at joinery, withdrew him to the kitchen to discuss improvements she had planned. I warmed to her for this, and so I think did Joel. She was a quite collected person, cool and blonde, straight-nosed and wearing something very plain I'd never wear—green linen— but all the same I sometimes wish I could. She talked about her daughters who were now away at school. I could see Pru measuring her for heroine's best friend in *See-Through Man*, with beady eye. But otherwise it had the promise of a fairly boring evening. All the same I quite like evenings without event. And boring people tend to make me feel I am a bit more interesting than I felt myself to be before I went to dinner with them.

Derek helped to supervise the final preparations of the meal (it seemed they shared domestic roles), while Gerry kept on pacing round the room with drink in hand. He also does, when standing still, this rocking on his feet, on tiptoe up and down again with snorts from time to time when waiting. He picked up *Horse and Hound* and threw it down again, then did the same with *Yachting Monthly*, although I know he's fairly interested in boats and seamanship. There was, I realised from the start, a danger that the feeling of establishment about the place might make both Joel and Gerry, Pru as well, express some very left-wing views and boast of Marxist principles, that sort of thing. Which is misleading since I have to say that all of us, when faced by someone to the left of us or someone more anarchical than we, can sound like staunch supporters of the Tory Party. Perhaps it would not be so boring after all.

It wasn't altogether drink that made the evening end the way it did, although we all had quite sufficient. I had brought as a gift a bottle of the turnip wine. Not very wise perhaps, but Derek picked it up and said: "Hey, this looks good."

I said: "It's rather new. I haven't tested it with my hydrometer as yet."

He had a sip and then another. Maybe that released his inhibitions, made him reckless in a way.

The meal was good. Expensive plain, but good. And Joel tucked in, and early conversation was along the lines of stories about holidays. The Savorys had recently returned from two weeks in Corfu. They'd rented somewhere Lawrence Durrell lived in years ago. And they described the scenery in glowing terms, perhaps intending to impress us with their literary sensibilities, as well as demonstrating their susceptibility to natural beauty. They also mentioned that they went to concerts sometimes, liked old films and theatre, and implied that they had not yet found in all their time so far in Yorkshire, people quite as civilised and cultured as ourselves.

Of course this all went down extremely well. Particularly with Gerry who soon began to reminisce about our ventures in the past, the Kirkby Overblow Festival of Anarchy, the poetry readings in the pubs, the happenings we brought about and many other lively times. "And does this still go on?" said Doreen handing round the profiteroles.

Gerry took a heap of these and said: "We've been a little lazy lately, haven't we?"

I looked at Joel and hoped that he might bring himself to mention that we had reformed, or maybe it would be more accurate to say revised our mode of life since then, and that, apart from meetings of 'New Pathways' and occasional forays into other poetry groups, we lived a quiet life now, attended to our crafts, were almost sober in existence. But Joel was gazing into Doreen's cleavage and had taken off his glasses for some reason. So his eyes were looking very brown and glowing in the evening sun which settled on their table silver and their bright white tablecloth. Doreen, well boned in linen dress, was smiling at him in a friendly fashion. I will say her throat and chest were very white. Surprising really: had she not sunbathed in Corfu much? She has a kind of English rose complexion which I envy—in a way.

Perhaps I should have spoken up at that stage, qualified the florid language Gerry used as he described our exploits of the past and put a spoke in his expansive boasts. Perhaps Pru should. I don't know why, since both of us, both Pru and I, are anxious to be factual and accurate, we let the men display the symptoms of wild living randiness.

Perhaps at heart—or not at heart but only sometimes—the two of us are rooted in acceptance of a minor role. Perhaps succeeding generations who have grown up feeling in themselves a woman's strength, will carry through and match their actions to their principles. At any rate last night there is no doubt we could have acted and prevented what occurred.

In retrospect I was surprised at Pru. She often speaks about concern that orgies are a touch provincial or suburban now. And, as for me, I mind an orgy less—no, let's be frank —I can enjoy it more when at the house of someone else. At home as hostess one feels too concerned that everyone is getting what they want.

One has to say just how it came about and answer questions like: who made the first move, who was second in enthusiasm? How did we get there to the king-size bed, the six of us? How did it happen that we split into two groups of three? And am I right in thinking that the drift upstairs began soon after Gerry said: "Let's all play Texas One-Card Showdown?"

It had got darkish in the Savorys' long fitted-carpet lounge by then. The cards were dealt and clothes came off. It takes some time with six. The person who receives the lowest card in every deal removes a garment or a watch, a sock, a necklace or an ear-ring. It isn't that unusual. Gerry got the idea from a film he saw. And if it has been seen by thousands on the screen, then you can bet a lot of people have been doing it. No wonder Pru gets worried that we could well be accused of commonplace activities. But Gerry has been on about this game for years between his bursts of purity.

The floor around their glass-topped coffee table soon was dotted round with piles of clothes. Some folded things as they

69

discarded them. Some threw them up into the air. I woke this morning with a vivid memory of Derek's tie which hung across a picture of the dental school in Liverpool that he has framed above his Yorkshire fireplace.

Twilight filtered weakly through their picture window, fell on flesh tones, dimpled knees and hairy shins. A sigh as Doreen let her Playtex bra fall down across her knees. A lot of giggles, laughs. I must not fool myself: I do remember shouting out in glee: "But Christ! I hardly know these people. Where am I?"

Dark as it was, you could see people giving sidelong glances as important parts of other people were revealed. I remember Derek shouting: "Who's for tennis now?" and vaulting over the back of the sofa of his three-piece suite, and Gerry in a tiny riding-hat but otherwise completely naked, trotting like a horse. And Joel stretched out along beneath the glass-topped table saying that he was the sleeping beauty and he needed raising with a kiss, which Doreen then bestowed on him.

I do remember details which I will not give. And maybe it's enough to say that Pru and I and Derek spent more time together while Joel and Gerry rolled about—and more—with Doreen. And I have to say that, though the Savorys both claimed this was their first time in a bed with more than two, they seemed to know exactly how to deal with what is quite a complicated process.

I kept an eye on Joel throughout. Drunk as I was, I know the part he played, and could chart every move he made. If this detracted from my own enjoyment, never mind. It's something that I always do. I listen for sweet nothings whispered into ears across the bed. I watch his hands, his eyes. And watched him even while the dentist's tongue was in among the teeth he'd crowned, and while my own, my tongue explored his perfect uncrowned canines, molars and incisors. And wondered fleetingly if he had broken any dentist's version of the hippocratic oath.

The contradiction is that here at this time all is flesh and yet one must suspend one's fleshly feelings and attend to what is going on around, consider feelings of the person next or under or on top. The mind for me does not give up. The social person hangs around, considers what it will be like when everyone exhausted lies back, struggles to the floor, retrieves a sock or wrapper, lights a cigarette and sees the dawn come up.

And as the dawn came up I looked across at Doreen who was lying there and gazing into Joel's face. He was asleep by then. I'd heard him marvel at her white flesh and seen him pillowed on her breasts. But since I'd had the heads of both Gerry and of Derek pillowed on my own and less substantial resting place, I wasn't going to grumble at him ever for tonight.

Gerry sees such moments as expressions of the vibrancy of life. Pru tells me he is much cheered by last night and quite himself again, "Depending on which self I mean. I'm so confused these days," she said.

"You're not the only one," I said, discussing the affair today.

"You sound a little doubtful?"

But in broad daylight as we let ourselves back into our house, a note was by the telephone in Bruce's writing: "Clo rang. Will ring again."

"For after all," says Pru, "if you are worried about contretemps as I well know you can be, just think: we might have played four-handed bridge instead of Texas One-Card Showdown, then someone would have been left out. We might have played at Scrabble but you get upset when beaten, don't you? Or Botticelli where a person thinks of someone who's alive or dead and other people have to guess. Last time we played at that remember you got all upset because we hadn't heard of King Wilhelm of Albania . . ."

"It isn't that," I said. "And anyway I checked. There was a King Wilhelm of Albania in 1922, I think it was . . ."

"And no one was upset or changed by it, last night I mean."

"I'm not upset at all," I said.

71

"And after all, you've finished having what you choose to call your complicated dental work. For heavens' sake we haven't many orgies left in us."

"That's true," I said. "That's very true."

When driving home I turned to Joel: "So was that good or was that good?"

"That's what we ask ourselves," he said.

"Oh don't feel guilty, darling heart. It's only a parenthetic set-back in what is a generally upward, onward trend . . ." But Joel had gone to sleep.

I drove south-east, the sun still low behind the trees and flashing at us crystalline through webs of leaves, or spearlike willows as we were beside the Wharfe, or rowans as we climbed a hill again. And Joel beside me, snoring now. Where had we been?

Seductive driving there where no cars seemed to be, where hedges came then dropped away, where sheep were grazing. Do they ever stop when nights are short like this? To think that everyone who crowded on these roads by day was now asleep in bed.

I left the main road, cut along the Roman road, along the flat run into town. And here on either side were tall Scots pines where crows nest, flying up to circle high above the car, and, since it is a road where cars go fast, you sometimes see a rabbit squashed and sometimes hares keep pace for yards and yards.

Joel groaned beside me, murmured in his sleep: "Three metres laminate and one point five mahogany." At least he seemed quite undisturbed.

A crow flew up across the windscreen, swooped above the dry stone wall and landed in a field. A rusty, wheelless and deserted car protruded from a ditch. Its door hung open, stuffing from upholstery burst out. Was this a tip or was this just a place where someone left a car that would not go?

Beyond the Scots pines there are fields beside the Roman road, but these are brownish, stony and unprofitable. Nothing grows on them. A cottage here and there with fallen roof, mid-field, exposed amid infertile space where no one ever walks.

Pru rang and said that she had got this plot idea, in which a woman has conceived when in a multi-sexual situation. Could I think of some way she could use it profitably?

Wednesday

When Clo was twelve or thirteen at the most she used to go to Youth Club where we lived—some miles away in fact. And James or I would fetch her home to our suburban comfort, so she would not have to walk a dark and tree-lined road. One night I quite forgot and so did James, for we were both preoccupied discussing his departure round the world and whether if he stayed away and for how long, divorce would be facilitatéd in the end.

I was about to say "Desertion makes it simpler in the end" when she walked in. She'd hitch-hiked from the main road in a lorry, so she said. The man was nice and only touched her on the knee and told her that his wife had left him not so long ago. He seemed quite sad, she said. She went to bed and we went on discussing separation when she'd kissed us both good-night. I think we scolded her a bit that she had failed to ring us up and remind us of our duties in her case.

I dreamed that scene last night, but in the colours Maurice dreams, in orange, flame, with khaki monsters swelling in and out and woke up late, the day half gone and sunlight showing round the curtains. And remembered Clo had rung last night. Got dressed and shouted on the stairs for Bruce. Got no reply. House empty so it seemed.

A letter on the mat:

Dear Monica, I hope to hear from you about the children's trip to Perpignan. The date is set—July 15th. And I forgot to mention in my last, the diamond ring I think you have. I hope that Clo can be entrusted with it ...

He ended as he always does by writing: 'That's all ... James'.

74

I sympathise with that. He cannot well put 'yours' or 'love from'. All the same I was a little miffed about the diamond ring. That ring is Clo's, I'm sure it was agreed.

'Dear James, I hope to send the ring via Clo . . .' but then I realised that I hadn't written back in answer to the letter which announced the marriage—or re-marriage rather.

'Dear James . . . I'm very glad to hear . . .' which sounded false and hypocritical.

'Dear James . . . That *is* good news . . .'

'Dear James . . . I note your news. The children will be with you on . . .' I could not promise that, however, so I put the letter on one side and went out shopping and the sun was out.

Just lately Joel has said I scuttle with my head poked forwards, shoulders bent. I say that is because in summer I would lose my hat so have to hold my head that way. He says I do it in the winter too. I say that is because in winter I wear hat and muffler too and they blow off if I stand up and face the wind.

Returning from the shop I noticed Bruce upon our open stairs, barefoot in his clean pink jeans and white shirt, carrying his sandals in his hand. "Just popping out," he said, "all right? Terry terza rima going O.K. then?" and ending as he always does with upward intonation of his voice. He does that even when he isn't asking questions.

"The what?" I said.

"I was trying to be quiet and not disturb you working."

"Well, you couldn't since I wasn't here."

"Or is it Harry haikus?" He was hopping on one foot to put his sandals on. "Or Vera villanelle? Is everything all right?"

"Clo rang last night?" I said.

"Oh yeah. She said she was O.K. She said to tell you that."

"Oh thanks. Did she say anything about . . . you know . . . Maurice?"

"Oh no, she didn't say a thing. Heyo! I'd better take the little bike." He pushed a lock of thin blond hair behind his ear and went to fetch Joel's Honda, then came running in again. "Forgot my sally stash," and went upstairs. I could see as he flashed past down the stairs again, the flattish wooden box which carried Bruce's marijuana.

I could have done with some of that. Joel only stipulates that Bruce refrains from smoking in the house, and Joel himself eschews it now, or rather has eschewed it now for several years. He had a bad trip after which he sat in bed and said, "So even bloody marijuana has now lost its savour."

But Bruce has let me have a little puff from time to time. We smoke outside, protected by the sunflowers and the sweetcorn. People in the recreation ground—the fence is lower there—are too involved in recreating to peer closer at the kind of cigarette we smoke. I say a little puff, but since I do not like to take too much from Bruce, I fill my lungs to bursting point and hold it there.

I'm rather worried about Bruce. He's not himself. I'm not sure what his true self is, but he is acting strangely, not attending college, that's for sure, although it is the end of term almost. Theresa rings and asks for him, but he is hardly ever here. I have an inkling that he has been playing golf with Ron. I dare not mention this to Barbara because she much resents Ron's stopping work for golf.

I tried to write to James again. Then wrote some more about my early life instead. I've sketched in wedding day in Isle of Wight. Perhaps I now should sketch in second wedding day. The ceremony was held at noon and after in the Lamb and Flag for sausage rolls and pie and peas. And Clo cried copiously, but only since she said she'd always heard that someone had to cry at weddings, and it was a lovely wedding, wasn't it? I don't remember much. Gerry wrote an ode, I think. Who came? Well—Pru and Gerry, Bob, of whom I have made mention early on this week, the Meadowcrofts— she is the secretary of New Pathways: he's a doctor. And the Sweets from down the garden centre, and my sister who left early to get a train back to Southampton for the boat across, and made it clear her presence was a token one. She did not welcome Bob's attentions. Jamie was not there, I think. He must have had to go to school.

Remember Jamie cried. Remember Clo whose boyfriend at the time was Kevin, who now runs the health food shop and sells me turmeric and wholemeal flour and lentils, green and red.

Just after that—a funeral. James's mother died. I did not go, but Clo went, taking Kevin, and she said she cried as much as at our wedding almost. And Jamie cried again, because he was too young to go. I sat and thought: 'It's ten past two; they will be in the church; it's half past two; they will be at the grave.'

I had not been that much in favour with the late-lamented, but about the time of the divorce we had begun to get on terms. Then, after when I used to drop the children at her door for visits, she would look at me with doubt as if she worried if she ought to kiss me now or not. We had been dis-related after all.

Pru says she's good friends with her ex. They meet in London when she goes to see her publishers. They laugh a lot about old times, she says.

Why James went off. I haven't covered that. He went to find himself. At that time I believed that this was possible. Though now I think you are the place you're at, which is the same as saying that you are the food you eat and is not inconsistent.

I picked his letter from this morning, held it and re-read it. His writing is shot through with curls and decorative swirls, developed not so long ago to give it character. A quality he feared he lacked. A fear, in my opinion not unjustified in my more calculating moments. Although a man who's walked in peace through wars in Israel, a coup d'état in Afghanistan and discussed the meaning of the meaning with a guru in Nepal, could not now be accused of lacking character perhaps.

Or maybe James went off after seeing the film of *Lawrence of Arabia*, again on television. Or maybe so that he could

77

grow his hair and wear one ear-ring in his ear like he had wanted to for years.

Remember James. Remember when he came one year, took Jamie out. They went to York and Jamie said: "He stood there in the Minster there by that big window at one end. He said it was like being in the mountains."

"He would have been referring to the feeling that one gets of being dwarfed," I said, "of being humbled. It is very natural."

As Pru would say when she's been reading Vonnegut a lot: "Well, so it goes."

I never got that letter written, though. Instead I wrote:

Tomorrow would have been our silver wedding day,
And in the morning or at any other time of day
You might just turn to her and say:
"That's funny. It's my silver wedding day today,
Or would have been."
And so might I.
To him.

I meet you only in the thick blood of our children's veins,
And through the bank politely.
That's all . . .
Monica.

I had arranged a little 'do' this coming Sunday. but Joel rang up this lunchtime, begging me to call this off.

"But darling heart! Pru says that you and Gerry, both of you, are on the short list for the Grassington Award. I have already phoned up people days ago."

"Please, precious, please. The times are out of joint."

"Fuck you, il penseroso," I said beneath my breath on putting down the telephone.

Sometimes on Sundays we have gatherings of friends. Selected carefully, we give them wine and salad, crusty bread and cheese. The idea was, the aim of social Sundays was to mix up artists from the different media. For instance there's a playwright whom we know just slightly who lives several roads away. I think he writes for television but I have not seen his work. We always say we'll watch, but then forget. He's been on Sundays here. And Gerry knows a man who is a potter. Pru knows one other novelist, but she comes from Darlington, which is rather far. And Ron and Barbara know a man who sculpts in chromium. And Clo brings friends, including Maurice, or she used to do.

Last time we had a Sunday Maurice drank too much and spent the afternoon beneath the broom bush which is in the centre of our little lawn. He lay out flat. His boots stuck up and tripped up Pru's friend from Darlington. I discovered later that she wrote romantic novels mostly set in hospitals, and I thought it odd that Pru approved of her: "She does have good technique," said Pru.

Our Sundays, though, are quite successful on the whole. There can be deep rifts of an aesthetic nature, such as the one which Gerry had with Mary Sweet—the garden centre lady—on the question: flower arranging—is it art? And much abuse was hurled across our crowded room. However many people think that scenes like that make for a better Sunday. They feel that something real has happened. At 2 p.m. today I started ringing round to cancel those we'd asked and polished up my Silver Wedding poem for a reading we were booked to do tonight.

"The trouble is with orgies, I've discovered," Pru said early on today, "you have to do a lot of mutual reassuring afterwards, but on the whole it had been good for us."

I looked at Gerry when we met tonight and he seemed calm enough. Quite reassured, I'd say, but less so Joel. I longed to be alone with him and comfort him. But that was not to be.

Because Joel sees that good art should be turned to making a good life, I had what I thought was a bright idea not long ago, suggesting that New Pathways Poetry Group should read our works in aid of charitable causes.

We advertised—and it is early days as yet—but so far only one good cause has asked for us. And thus I found myself tonight awaiting, in a parish room, my turn to read. There were just four of us: Joel, myself and Gerry, also Suzy Meadowcroft who is, I should just mention here, a buxom lady given to a lot of phallic imagery in verse.

Joel looked around in some dismay. The audience was small and mostly old. I'd dressed with care. I thought Joel would read extracts from his *Two In One*. Since this is dedicated to me, I need to look the part as far as possible. I'm idolised in *Two In One*, the perfect woman, so I had put on my pinkish rainbow skirt and lacy blouse with bishop sleeves. I also wore some jewellery; a batch of Indian silver bracelets, a locket with a crescent set in rubies and my rings: Joel's amethyst and James's single diamond, but I'd kept the latter on as much to keep it safe as anything.

I always feel a little proud to walk with Joel into a room where we are reading, say, and see heads turn and hold my own up high. And when I sit and he is reading *Two In One* I cast my eyes down modestly. I was prepared for this, and hopeful too. His voice would reassure me, and the 'oohs' and 'ahs' and cooings which issue from audiences for *Two In One*, would build him up. He had a hunted look, however, as he sat beside me in the front row of the little parish room the other side of town. He'd rushed home, had no time to change and had but pecked at food.

I have to say the people we are reading to tonight were not, at best, attentive to our efforts. The Friends of St Winifred's Old Folk's Club were restless during Suzy Meadowcroft's long piece about the Embley Moor Television Mast. And in *The Water Snake*, a woman yawned and many people's dentures clicked.

Then it was Gerry's turn. He read *A Journey on the North Yorks Railway*, about the old steam line which runs from Pickering to Whitby. They seemed to like that ballad form, but then a man stood up and asked why Gerry left out Goathland station where the train stops nearly every time it runs. And Gerry wouldn't answer him, but stumped back to his chair and sat a little sulkily I thought and kept on looking at his watch.

Perhaps it would be best, I thought, if I missed out my turn. That would give Joel a longer time to read. And so I folded up my Silver Wedding poem and some others that I'd brought with me and put them in my bag, and when Joel called my name to read I nodded, signifying that I thought it better if he followed Gerry to the space beside the table, chair and glass of water, all of which the Chairman of the Old Folk's Club had thoughtfully set up. Joel stood up, cleared his throat and started on the early stanzas of his work *Children, Animals and Idiots.*

Oh Joel! I thought. Oh dear! It must be said that this is not an easy piece. Not easy on the ear. It gives a dour and sombre picture of the present day, of high-rise flats and children grey with lack of sun. It draws on garish places, queues and blowing paper bags on dusty corners of a street, of mothers' faces turned away to Bingo Halls. It uses words like gristle, snot and spit. It was not wise of Joel to read that poem, I'm afraid. Not wise at all. The woman next to me, who had been nodding off quite peacefully, sat up and buttoned up her cardigan and listened in alarm. A youngish couple just behind sat forward concentrating hard. And Gerry got his Restless Leg, a syndrome that's to do with acids in the circulation, a kind of cramp for which he takes salt pills. He took a phial of these and swallowed some and some ran on the floor and rolled towards Joel's feet.

And this just at the moment Joel had reached the lines which give the essence of the work. Joel reads this with an apocalyptic air. He strides about and reads, walks up and down and knows a lot of it by heart, of course. He'd reached the bit where lightning strikes a tower block and a crack appears in concrete and a fire breaks out and small black figures, stick-like, hurtle down to broken paving stones. A horde of boys on skateboards shoot away, a girl with lilting

81

step, not looking back, trips off and gets into a large black car and many other evil and symbolic images.

A salt pill crunched beneath his foot. Joel stopped and turned. It wasn't Gerry whom he seemed to gaze upon, but all the faces in the hall. And what he saw there made him sit and lean his elbows on the table and put his head down in his hands.

We waited. Was he ill? Perhaps the others thought he'd finished anyway. The man who'd questioned Gerry on the matter of the Goathland station stood up, saying, "Ah no, young lad, you've got it wrong . . . Ah no, things aren't as bad as that these days. There's many of us better off than ever we have been," and he described the luxury in which his son lived and compared it to the hovel in which he himself had spent his childhood days.

I was about to get up, go to Joel, but then the girl behind me stood. She claimed—if art intended to enhance, then what did Joel think he was aiming at by castigating youth and modern aspirations in this way? How could the youth, the people of her age see any point in going on in Joel's dark universe? "What hope, I ask you, for the unborn child?" I turned my head a little way and saw that she was pregnant by about four months perhaps. Joel looked across at me as if to plead with me to come to his assistance. "And you didn't even mention adventure playgrounds," said the girl.

Her husband said: "And what about Suzuki violin teaching then?"

"I am quite wrong, of course," said Joel.

The girl said "No, of course you're not completely wrong. It's just a feeling of discomfort that your poem gives. Your picture of the present day goes all one way . . . it is unbalanced, as I'm sure you will agree."

Joel's fists were white and clenched. I felt his hatred and his disappointment. Pru says I suffer far too much on his behalf, but I'd have been inhuman not to empathise with him tonight and share with him the feeling of rejection. My stomach clenched in sympathy with his, was filling with that same sharp adrenalin which would be pumping into his.

"I *am* completely wrong," he said. "The world is pretty, full of flowers and sun and babbling streams . . ."

"Do you have children of your own? If so . . ." the girl began to say.

Joel did not answer her and so I interrupted her on his behalf: "One does not have to have direct experience . . ."

Joel held his hand aloft as if to ask me to be quiet, as if there was no point in countering such futile challenges.

"My grandson has a brand new motorbike," the old man said. "They go for holidays abroad each year . . ."

The woman in the cardigan, unbuttoned now again, described a pony that her great-niece had. "In that case," Joel said, clutching at his stomach, rocking now, "no one here needs charity, and we, who hoped to give it, are not wanted here." He looked across at me as if to say I'd landed him here in this paltry place specifically to be attacked by idiots the like of which he wrote about. And I had hoped that this would cheer him up, this effort at the spreading of our art, my little plan. And here he was rejected, childless and with stomach pains.

At that point Gerry leaned towards me, right across the woman in a cardigan who sat between us, and he whispered, "Read! For God's sake, read."

My voice was choked. I had to clear my throat at least three times. I started on the Silver Wedding poem, then read *Calder Willow*, an early work I have not much conviction in, and finished with the Ode to Clo upon her sixteenth birthday. I don't know quite how long I read, but as my voice croaked out I sensed a movement in the hall, and felt I read to many empty chairs, and when I finally sat down where Joel had sat in pain, not many minutes earlier, he'd disappeared.

"We should have made him stay to fight," said Suzy Meadowcroft.

She's larger than I am—by several inches (several stones as well)—and so I drew myself to my full height and said:

"You may be hot on phallic imagery, but men themselves, their egos, are your weak point, Suzy Meadowcroft..." and was about to add that Terence Meadowcroft, her husband, looked as though his ego never had a chance, poor man. But Gerry interrupted me: "I'll go and find him, Monica."

"Not so!" I said, and pushed right past him, Suzy Meadowcroft and the lady chairman of the Friends who had invited us. I found myself outside. He'd left the car. I took this, driving down this tree-lined road where streetlights flickered and went dim, then bright again, and slowed to let my headlights pick out figures walking. None of them was Joel, however. I took the road he'd walk, down into town and up again, and by the Lamb and Flag I thought a figure that I saw was him, but no . . .

Our street deserted, curtains drawn. Our house was dark and so was next door dark. I knew that Ron and Barbara had left earlier to go down to the Hofbrauhaus in Leeds with friends they'd made when on their Adriatic Cruise.

Our room was warm from daylight sun, and having switched the lamp beside the table on, I opened out the garden door, but closed the curtains at the front. I took the silver chain from round my neck and dropped the locket on the table, curled the chain around it in a circle. The long oak table made by Joel, an early work, but sound and deeply polished, beeswaxed first. I gazed into its depths and wondered if he'd left before I read the Silver Wedding poem, or whether, hearing that, he'd felt it cool in tone. Oh no! It wasn't that. I understand my Joel, he me, I think.

'I first met Joel'—I wrote upstairs. When did I first meet Joel? He'd been there always as they say. "That's anima meets animus," said Pru when we were talking of these matters once. "It feels like cataclysmic force, however, but you have to work it through, which can take years and years and years." She has been in analysis from time to time. "It's best if you can meet your animus when young. It happens quicker then, so by the time you're thirty, say . . ."

Some heavy footsteps in the road, which stopped outside our house. I switched the lamp off, stood and looked outside. Beside the streetlight opposite stood Maurice very still, arms folded on his chest. From up here you could see his hair was getting thin on top.

I could not see to write: 'I first met Joel. I saw him coming down the street with well-known poet Gerry McLeHose. He does look nice, I thought of Joel, and so we met . . .'

A sound downstairs. I moved towards the landing, stood and listened, hearing nothing now. Ears strained, received a rushing silence. That was all. Some distant shouts, some very distant traffic. What exactly was that sound downstairs just now? The garden door—I'd left it very slightly open, hadn't I? A click? A thump? A sound which must have been familiar in some way, which signified an entry or return. I looked out of the window once again. The lamp-post was deserted now. I had not heard him move and yet those heavy footsteps are quite unmistakable.

The top of stairs again. I stood there looking down. The lamp was on down there. I'd left it on. I could just see the window to the garden too. A moth flapped round the lamp and threw a hectic shadow on the window seat and walls.

Light footsteps coming up the road. Young Ashley from next door was arm in arm with beautiful Lorraine. The streetlight showed her hair was auburn and she wore a pale blue dress. She bent her neck and this was very white, as necks of red-haired people are. They stopped and crossed the road and took the garden path to number forty-four. I heard the door shut after them.

The churchbell several roads away began to chime. The telephone began to ring. The bell struck ten. I held the pillar of the banisters and waited for return of silence. Then I would go down.

Some music from next door. Young Ashley playing tapes to young Lorraine. A car came up the road. I could not move. Moths, more than one, now slapped around the lamp with thuds. Considered: if it's Maurice, he is harmless, isn't he?

85

He could have gone on down the road and through the recreation ground and walked along the backs and climbed our fence. It's he who needs the help, not I.

A pause and then the telephone again. Visions of Clo in seaside box or Joel from who knows where or Jamie even over at the camp, or Bruce, or yet Theresa ringing ringing thinking why is that house empty? I leaned a little forward to see more. The table I could see, one end of it, but not the end with bracelets, rings and locket on. No shadows other than the shifting bashing ones the moths made on the wall and window end.

Remembered night when Clo was out. A man said: "Will you baby-sit for me? My wife's in hospital. I have to go and see her now. My children are alone." "Oh yes," said Clo and ran beside him up the road. And later in his house: "Well, are you going to see your wife? And where are those children that you spoke about?" Came running home: "I've had what you might call a narrow squeak."

The music from next door had stopped. Faint voices. Ashley and Lorraine in clinch unable to change tape? Decided: move one foot to next floorboard. Gently does it. Move next foot to further board, then turn. A long way to the bedroom door. Clo's room was nearest now. Her door has lock on it. I'd sit down there with back to door. Slow motion, sit. Safe now, decided.

No light to see the dust which clings to Hindu bells, although a little light shone on the glass-framed picture of her father in his Air Force uniform, and on one side of it, one of the Beatles which she also framed. There was a source of light in there. So was it starlight or was it from the crib she got at Sunday School and which is painted luminous? It came from Hong Kong at a time when luminosity equalled radio-activity. Fiendish Chinese! I said, and wrenched it from her little grasp, but could not bring myself to burn it quite. I hunched my feet beneath my skirt and felt the dust of Clo's neglected floor. I held the crib and smothered all its light by holding it beneath my skirt.

Thursday: a.m.

"The trouble is," said Clo, "the seagulls deafen you by day. I tried to ring last night. They wheel around all day and Keith and Nina feed them on the cliff, which is amazing. Suddenly a thousand gulls—well, not a thousand quite— appear from nowhere so it seems. In fact of course they're perched on rocks and rooftops or they're strutting in the fields, and one calls out and then another hears and then they all sweep down . . ."

"You will be coming home?" I said.

"I will, but it's like Hitchcock's *Birds* here . . ."

"Then you and Jamie can go off together . . ." Seagull cries crescendoed. Clo said: "Wait a minute, I will try and close the door. The wind is getting up. I've got a great idea . . ."

"Hey, Clo." A rushing on the line and then her voice returned. "You there? There is this bloke that Keith and Nina know. He's French. He's called Michel and fishes in the bay. Now he goes home each Friday to St Malo. His boat is gorgeous by the way. It's painted green. The sort of cabin thing is yellow and it's called *Mon Rêve*." The seagulls called again. "The trouble is the door—it keeps on blowing and the twins are just outside. You know—Keith and Nina's twins . . . they're two. They had a birthday just the other day. We made a cake. They're just outside—it's risky for them on the cliff . . ."

I could hear human voices too and then a distant bang. Clo said: "I think there's been a wreck. That was a rocket went up in the sky. They call it the maroons. There's just a puff of smoke. That means the lifeboat will be going out. I'll have to take the twins . . ."

"But, Clo, just tell me, please . . ."

87

"It's bedlam here. I mean it is incredible. There's people rushing past. You see the lifeboat men drop everything and get in cars and drive like mad. A lift goes down into the boat-house, and if you . . ."

"But who's Michel?"

"I'd hitch to Perpignan, but only if you could send Jamie on his own or by some other route. I mean they keep an eye on kids in planes . . ." It was as if her voice was carried by the wind. Or maybe it was like when coming round from dentist's gas you hear a voice and then it fades away until you hear another voice. It seems that if you hurry down the causeway just below the telephone kiosk, you see the lifeboat shoot out of its shed and with a siren or alarum shrilling. Then you see it touch the sea, a crest of, plume of water curls on either side. The men wear yellow oilskins and sou'westers. If she took the twins and hurried down . . .

"Oh yes. That does sound quite exciting, Clo, but when does Michel mean to go . . . I mean."

"He's super. Very big, not weedy like some Frenchmen are . . . and Keith says . . ."

A clicking on the line and then the dialling tone. It wasn't that her money had run out because the call had been transferred. I was prepared for this. I'd written down the number on our codebook. But since I had not got my glasses on I could not read the number which was fairly long. By the time I rang again she must have left the box. It seems the rush down to the lifeboat in summer when the visitors are there is hectic. Keith who takes an interest in local matters, takes an RNLI money box and does quite well.

I waited, dialled again. The time, I think was 9 a.m.

She's travelled on the Continent before. She's wandered at some time through many countries of the EEC. But it is people whom she bears in mind, not places. She will say "I met this bloke" and I say "Where?" and she says "Rome or somewhere or it may have been Vienna, I don't know, but he . . ." and then she will describe his looks, his thoughts, beliefs, his family down to aunts and uncles, all the people

88

that he's met, the books he's read. But if I say "But where does he come from?" she says "Oh, somewhere in the States, I think, or Canada", and then she says "He's got one leg" or mentions that he is at any rate disabled, and I say "How did that happen?" and she says "He must have been in some disaster somewhere or a war . . ."

I went to fetch the atlas out of Jamie's room and opened it. The map of France was scribbled over, marked off not in provinces but written on in black felt pen, here Burgundy, here Chartreuse, there Meuse. I found St Malo, and the southern coast of England was marked in as well. And there the Channel Islands in between, and many outer rocks of these on which I've heard ships founder.

A glassy heat, intensifying green. Pru rang about the novel once again. My motherhood: did I remember saying once, she said, that I had always worried more about my children's health and safety than about their morals on the whole.

"Did I say that?" I said.

She said: "You used to be amazed you said, that you could keep them fit and thriving and alive."

"I'm not sure now. I mean I didn't think about the morals much when they were babies, but you wouldn't, would you?"

Pru went on very business-like. I guessed that she was asking written questions: "Question two," she said, "and would you say that maybe in the 'fifties and the 'sixties, there was such a sense of optimism abroad about the basic innocence of human nature, you might say, that then it seemed that teaching morals was superfluous?"

"Well, in the 'fifties mostly, Pru," I said, "I worried more about the bomb in any case. I didn't think we'd live to recognise the fruits of rearing children anyway."

"I think that we must leave that on one side for now," said Pru.

"Most people do nowadays."

"You didn't force your morals on them, then?"

"I used to hit them sometimes, though. I used to hit them

hard," I said. "I lunged at them and shouted and I screamed and still do sometimes if I had them here to lunge at, shout at, scream at . . ."

"All right," Pru said. "Thanks. Well, I hope you're feeling better soon."

I noticed that a breeze moved sunflower heads. They shook and strained against the string which held them up. The bamboo canes inclined and one gave out and then another. String came loose, heads lolled. I ran outside. And shouted out across the fence. "They won't fly that balloon if it gets rough!"

But Barbara didn't answer me. She'd washed a row of yellow dusters, hung them on the line. Her day for duster-washing is a Friday.

"Have you heard from Nicola?"

She shook her head and pinned another duster to the line. I did not think I'd better ask if they'd enjoyed themselves last night. For very late I'd heard their voices raised through our adjoining bedroom wall. Some trouble at the Hofbrauhaus perhaps?

"We might get rain," I called, but she had gone inside again. A cooling breeze, a current in the air, a draught across the recreation ground, a bluster almost, one which made the yellow dusters dance out horizontally and caused our garden door to bang and bounce upon its latch.

I write on Sunday now. The reason for the gap in writing will emerge. I have to say Joel came home late. I have to say both he and Bruce who came in with him for reasons which I cannot yet descry, arrived at 1 a.m. both very much the worse for wear.

I had been dozing in Clo's room. I heard the motorbike and went downstairs and saw them sway beside the garage door and went outside and saw that Bruce had been unwell. And Joel was holding on to him and saying: "That's right, Bruce, old lad, that's right," while Bruce complained he was about to die. And Joel was telling him he was a marvel:

90

"You're a marvel, Bruce," while Bruce threw up again along the path beside the house.

They lay there, both of them upon the floor. Quick as a flash I fetched a bucket each. Then bathed Joel's brow and took his glasses off and said, "Oh speak to me, my darling," several times. He groaned and said how much he loved me at that moment. I was perfect; that is what I was.

"You mustn't be offended by those silly people, darling heart." I sniffed his breath, smelt Theakston's Old Peculiar and guessed that he had been down to the late-night drinking club with Bruce.

"I've told them, haven't I?" he said to Bruce. "Bruce knows how marvellous you are."

Bruce rushed upstairs and reached the bathroom just in time. I threw the bucket after him: "You've had him at the Ivy, haven't you!" I called.

I fetched a blanket, covered Joel and sat and watched him breathe with what seemed effort, held his hand and reassured him that I was not angry with him, not at all.

We thought the Ivy was a good place once. We went to meet our friends, discuss the yins and yangs of life and current trends in art. It was a nice fresh pink inside with pale green pastel plastic ivy leaves. And there were small round tables, glass-topped, where we'd put our glasses. We could drop in any time. A touch art-deco which was coming in again and had not reached collectors yet.

At first we welcomed younger folk. After all, a café society had to stay alive with new blood, new ideas. But soon the younger ones outnumbered us, outdrank us too. A lot were under age. Then Clo began to come. At first I used to pretend I didn't see her there and hoped Joel wouldn't see her either.

Quiet-spoken, murmuring, peaceful. Then more of them until one night we found our table taken. Joel said: "What they say is not that interesting, I've noticed."

"Perhaps it's up to us to lead and make it interesting," I said.

Pru said: "The birth rate, I have read, in 1959 began to climb and climb. These are the multitudes who feel they ought to have a share in lotus-eating, I suppose."

"They smell," said Joel, "and don't pick up their feet when walking much."

The place became less clean. One night a fight broke out and food was thrown. The Ivy hit the headlines: 'Man throws ham and egg at wife.' The food stayed on the wall for several weeks. It made us feel a little queasy there. Joel saw something floating in his beer.

A disco opened up downstairs for under-eighteens. Children gathered on the wall outside like swallows, and an ice cream van began to call. 'Watch out for children' was the writing on the van.

"Have you noticed?" Joel said thoughtfully, "that is ambiguous."

A girl of twelve or so called out: "Hullo four eyes." Joel clutched my hand and said we must stop going there, and so we never went again. Until that night that he came home at one.

I thought next morning I would find him in bed beside me. I predicted he would creep upstairs as dawn came up and lie there groaning maybe in contrition. But early on I came downstairs to see. It was a bit like that first Easter Day: the tomb was empty and the blanket thrown back on the floor. Beside all this a note said 'I love you very much'.

'What day is this?' I thought and heard myself speak out aloud, "The times are out of joint", and this reminded me to go and look for Bruce, but he had gone as well.

I held Joel's note: 'I love you very much', and yet for two days we had hardly been alone or spoken very much at all. It used to be like that with James because on Monday evenings he played squash, on Tuesdays went to rugby training. Wednesday was the Young Conservatives (and later on the Churchill Club) and Thursday was, if I remember right, Round Table (later the Rotarians). Friday we kept for friends, although we didn't have a lot, and Saturdays was rugby (cricket in the summer), Sunday visiting his mother out at Harrogate.

Who was it said the truth about Othello was that he and Desdemona never consummated? The theory being that he went ahead to Malta straight after the wedding, and when she joined him there, Iago had already started rumours.

Clo's Hindu bells were chiming wildly as I tried to work upon a poem which began:

The times are out of joint
For me, but somewhere on a peak
With wind in hair, she looks out,
Seagulls overhead. For her, life starts . . .

I went to close her window, saw across the recreation field wind fan along the massy tops of trees, approaching ripple which in time reached grass where not mown short, and made this pale as if a light passed over it.

A girl called Zoe came. At first I thought that this was Sylvia again—the one who came on Tuesday. This Zoe looked about the same size and had curly hair and wore a short fur coat. She said that she and John, her boyfriend, had been up with Maurice all the night.

"Oh dear," I said.

"He nearly knocked out John," she said, "because we kept a hold of all his pills and things."

"There's always the Samaritans," I said.

"They don't do much," she said, "just send you to the doctor."

I turned the television on. A weather forecast might be shown mid-afternoon perhaps. Instead there was a silent undulating sea (I'd turned the sound right down) with little sprays of spume, and men, all black and greased with oil, were clinging to a life-raft. But one, who might have been their officer and might have been John Mills beneath the oil, looked up with hand to shade his eye at lowering skies. "What happened to the other girl?" I said. "To Sylvia?"

"Oh, she got fed up, too. Now me and John have got to go . . ."

"Samaritans," I said, "or doctors . . . who's his doctor?" I watched a man slide off the raft from weakness, hands which slipped while other hands reached out like God's to Adam on the Sistine chapel ceiling. Lightning flashed across the television sky. The one they lost bobbed off away, his head lolled back. He floated in his life-jacket, was lost beyond the peak of yet another rolling wave.

"He tells the doctor that he needs more pills," said Zoe.

"His parents then . . ."

"I tried to ring them up. Last night. They would be at the pub, he said."

"You might try ringing out of opening hours."

"He doesn't get on with his parents, but he still wants Clo."

"I think," I said, and bent to turn the television off, "I think that Clo is possibly in France. Or on the way there . . ."

She took her coat off, put it on the couch beside her. The fur was matted at the collar. Underneath she wore a floppy dress with flouncy skirt and T-shirt over it. However, it is most unfair of me to criticise the way she looked when she had had, it seemed, a most traumatic night. She was telling me how John, her boyfriend, should have started work today.

"What is his job?"

"Oh, something at the Social office down in Leeds," she said. "They got fed up with finding jobs for him and gave him work themselves."

I found this very interesting. I stood up, looked out of the window to peruse the sky for signs of breaking storms. But then I re-arranged my thoughts. I must remind myself she had not come to discuss the ethics of employment policy at the social security office, but the fate of Maurice at this moment.

The girl was sitting at the table now. Perhaps she wanted to be nearer me, to emphasise a point. "It has to be his parents, doesn't it?"

"He hasn't touched his books at all. He's gone right off."

The sun was out, however, still. This window faces west and clouds had piled above the odd numbers, thick and white. "He's gone off what?"

"Astrology."

"Oh yes, he would have, wouldn't he? I mean they do. I mean you could just call the doctor. Don't send Maurice there, but get the doctor to come out and make him see . . ."

"It is a her, the doctor is."

"Then she would understand."

"It doesn't make much difference, does it, which it is, a him or her."

"Perhaps not," and I thought perhaps in times of stress it should not ever matter which. "You'd do it for a child," I said, "you'd call the doctor for a child."

"He's twenty-one."

I knew his age; he had a birthday not so long ago, his twenty-first, and at the time I marvelled since he seemed to me an ageless lad.

Then Zoe went and wandered back along the avenue like Sylvia had two days before. I waved and shut the door and sat there at the table where she'd sat, and looked towards the telephone.

It seems an anticyclone centred over Jutland is at work to keep the western storms at bay, and east coast holiday resorts will have the best of it today, tomorrow and the weekend through, although it's possible some freakish tongues of turbulence may just reach out beyond the Pennines and bring rotten weather to some spots predicted as remaining sunny.

I took the green string from my pocket and some scissors and I cut enough to tie each sunflower near the top. I did it slowly and with care because the sunflowers at their stakes reach higher than the fence-top and can be quite easily seen from Barbara's side. "Do you know many people who've committed suicide?" I called across the fence.

Barbara was wearing rubber gloves and washing down their Spanish garden furniture. "The man down at the corner

95

shop," she said. "It didn't work." She leaned back on her knees and squeezed a cloth into a plastic bowl. "Ron's Uncle Frank. He tried. He failed as well."

I tied a knot to anchor one head firmly to the stake, and then I pushed the stake some inches deeper in the ground. The string flapped up and down. I cut it short.

"The man who runs the corner shop in Phyllis Road, you know the one that opens all day Sundays, not the man who runs it now but the one who used to run it just before the man who runs it now—he took a chair and then a rope and put it round the bacon hook they used to hang the sides of bacon from . . ."

Firm, steady now, this sunflower head, although its leaves blow up as if they were a collar round its neck to frame its face. I stood quite high upon the garden bench and saw repeated all along the garden backs uncounted flutterings and noddings.

The man who used to run the corner shop in Phyllis Road had got the rope around the hook and then jumped off the chair and then the hook came out. Barbara squeezed the cloth and wiped the grooves between the claws on which their garden table rests. "You can still see the socket where the hook came out. It's just above the freezer in the shop. They got the freezer after that. They keep the bacon in the freezer now. It was just after VAT came in. He got behind . . ."

"Behind?"

"Behind with working out his VAT."

While Barbara talked about the suicides she'd known, attempted ones, I tightened up the final sunflower stalk and heard the metal swings beside us in the recreation ground begin to squeak, and yet with no one swinging them. She raised her head and looked up to the sky and put a shielding hand up to her eyes. "Ron's Uncle Frank—he tried. They got the stomach pump to him. He says that if you do it, do it proper, Ron, he said. It's that degrading having stomach pumps, he said. Ron's Uncle Frank has always been a queer one though," she said. "Not queer like we say queer but strange, outlandish, you could say. His mother threw herself into the Nidd, Good Friday once. She was religious like and thought she'd rise again come Sunday maybe."

"The mother of Ron's Uncle Frank. That must have been Ron's Grandma then?"

"No. His Uncle Frank married his father's sister, married Ron's Auntie Rose."

"So not related really then?"

"He was his *Uncle* Frank," said Barbara.

I hope I haven't made it seem that Barbara's voice is raucous as she calls across the fence. It's light and musical and nearly accentless. Her intonation is a Yorkshire one. That's all.

The local paper gives the number. Over this it says 'Worried? Desperate? Lonely?' That afternoon quite late I rang. A woman asked my name. I said it didn't matter. It was not my name that mattered. It was Maurice and I tried to give her the address. "But tell me *your* name, dear."

"It's not me, it is Maurice I am ringing for, and my name doesn't matter."

"I have to call you something. You're in trouble and I need to have a name to call you by."

"I'm not in trouble. I . . ."

"But all the same . . ."

"All right. It's Monica."

"Well, Monica, that's better, isn't it?"

The sunflowers now were straight, upstanding. It must have been quite late because the schools were out. I could see children on the swings. From there, inside the house, you cannot see the swings themselves, the stands of them, but only children's heads as they come up above the fence, then disappear, and then their feet swing into sight and then their heads again.

"It has to be the client who reports," the woman said.

"The client won't report. I am reporting for him. I know he needs help and it could be urgent."

"Is he a member of your family?"

"No . . . just a . . . friend."

"I see." Her voice went distant and I thought she might have put her hand across the telephone and be speaking to another person. "You're involved with him?" she said.

"No, I am not. My daughter is or rather was . . ."

"Now, Monica. I'm going to have to ring you back. Now stay right there. I think your doctor is the one to help you out . . ."

I said: "It isn't anything to do with me. I mean it *is*, but on the other hand . . ."

"Now, Monica . . ."

A car drew up outside. I heard the door slam, footsteps coming round the house and Gerry's face peered in the window. In fact he pressed his face against the window pane and flattened out his nose and put his hands up to his ears and wagged his fingers.

"Now Monica. Now listen, Monica. In case I have to ring you back I'd like to have your number . . ."

"But I only want to know," I said, "if there is any way, if Maurice won't report himself . . ."

"If you could bring him to the phone . . ."

"He isn't here . . ."

"I thought you said . . ."

"I mean it only is to do with me in as much we are all to do with everyone we know . . . He doesn't understand himself that's what it is . . ."

"Do *you*?"

"Well, I don't know him all that well but my analysis of the situation is . . ."

"But Monica, I wonder if you understand your*self* . . ."

Behind me Gerry, who had walked in through the garden door, was sitting at the table, looking at my terza rima notes, having pulled them out towards him. Then he pushed them back and sat there with his head in hands. Then drummed his fingers. I put the phone down, sat there, saying nothing, thinking maybe I should have told them that he, Maurice, was my son-in-law. I'm sure they do good work. I'm sure that many lives are saved, much agony alleviated, anguish eased. I'm sure that someone somewhere, some nice woman with a bit of time on hand and a feeling for the contact with distressed humanity, is wondering who were Monica and Maurice and what she could have done to ease the desperation which she's advertised to ease.

That afternoon quite late, I sat there with Gerry at the table, looking at him, hearing that he spoke but knowing nothing that he said. Then Joel came home. I watched the two of them outside and heard their voices. I think I made a cup of tea for them and turned the weather forecast on again.

Thursday: p.m.

I lay there in the back of Barbara's open car and watched the greyish sky speed by. Or rather we were speeding past beneath the scudding blackish clouds, and sometimes Barbara's long white silk-knit scarf was blown back like a banner in between me and the clouds. Pru sat in front, dark glasses on and black rain hat, although it never seemed to rain that day. We took a long straight road, and if I sat up I could see the tops of hills in profile and I wondered if, had I been dropped here in the middle of this stretch of landscape, parachuted down, I would have guessed exactly where I was.

"Turn left," I heard Pru say and felt the car lurch to one side, and then I heard her say: "This is ridiculous, this really is."

A flat land this. This road shot east between rich fields of corn still green in places, poppies at the edge of every field. And every now and then a brick-red village came, and here a silo up beside a farmhouse, there a tractor working late on hay.

"This is absurd," said Pru again, "turn right." She had been saying how absurd it was, it seemed, for hours. Perhaps it was absurd. But I had ceased to argue that it was a gesture of solidarity with Barbara, whose idea it was to come.

Every now and then a glider stood above us framed against the sky and seemed immobilised. On those occasions I sat up and looked behind to see if it had landed in a field. I'd taken off my hat for fear it would be blown away and then I'd have to say to Barbara: "Stop! I've lost my hat!" But Pru was holding hers with one hand to her head. She had the map upon her knees and somehow at the same time smoked a long thin Dutch cigar which kept going out.

Of all the three of us, I reckoned Barbara was best dressed for the occasion, looking part and parcel of the long low car, with headscarf staying firmly on her head and belted mac. We bumped a little on a hump-back bridge. "That was the River Swale, I think," said Pru.

I mused that women in pursuit look rather silly when they are not dressed for it. They're handicapped because of clothes. Or maybe women in pursuit look silly anyway. I wished I'd had a chance to change to trousers and my khaki shirt. I wished that urgency allowed one time to change before one set out on adventures. But was quite glad at that stage that I'd kept my hair old-fashioned, straight and fairly short. In spite of Pru's black hat, hers kept blowing out. The perm she had not long ago had gone like crazy corkscrews standing out around the edges of her hat.

To start with I'd been in the front. But somewhere around Boroughbridge Pru said that she was feeling queasy and we stopped and changed our places in the car.

Perhaps, I mused, it was like this in war-time bomber crews. Pru navigator, Barbara pilot, me rear gunner. Maybe if there was another war, or maybe if active feminism had pre-dated World War Two, we might have found ourselves in such a situation. Pru often says she'd vote for female conscription any time, but doesn't dress like it. She says that when I wear my khaki shirt and coffee-coloured trousers I look a bit like someone the Israeli army wouldn't take.

The journey had begun around half-seven, maybe later— eight o'clock perhaps. For that was when the mounting tension burst in Barbara's breast. Since seven we'd been sitting there, just women without men, a peaceful scene except that Pru was pacing up and down and saying that she'd always sworn she'd never spend a moment in this fashion in her life again: "Domestic! Yuccy! Women without men."

"But many feminists believe this is the way ..." I half began to say.

"I'm not a nihilist," she said.

101

I should have questioned that. I'm sure she got that wrong. But then I get confused with different strands of women's politics. But Barbara, who was knitting half way up an Arran knit for Ashley, was at that stage, so it seemed, resigned to waiting and was talking of the time before when Gerry, Joel and Ron stayed away all night.

"You mean the time they went to Whitley Bay?" I said.

"The time they *said* they went to Whitley Bay," she said.

"The time they said they hadn't come home late because you had a migraine and you must not be disturbed..."

"The time they *said* they hadn't come home late because I had migraine."

It's doubtful why Pru came around. She said it was to get more details for her novel. She was worried she'd offended me. She had this problem still about the room in which adultery was committed.

"You could just try not mentioning which room they're in," I said.

"I've thought of that," said Pru. "You say that Gerry came at five?"

"About that time," I said. "I didn't talk to him. He talked to Joel. Then sort of disappeared..." I thought a bit and then said: "Barbara, you know they *did* bring back a stick of rock that time. It did have Whitley Bay right through because I ate mine and..."

"I told Ron what to do with mine," said Barbara. Then she sighed and started on another row of knitting, flicked the wool up round her little finger. Ron like Joel had missed his tea. But worse than that he'd missed the Thursday session which they always have to do the VAT. "What's more," said Barbara, "the Vatman will be round tomorrow..."

"So then the shit will hit the fan," said Pru. "Why don't you do it on your own? And show him you can manage very well without him just for once?"

And Barbara sighed again. I told Pru, hoping she would get the message and desist from urging Barbara on to greater recklessness, that the man down at the corner shop may well

102

have tried to hang himself because of failings in completing paper work for VAT.

Then Barbara rolled her knitting up, speared the ball with needles, put it in the knitting bag and went to fetch her best white mac and scarf and, belted, stood before us saying she was off.

"They won't be at the Lamb and Flag," Pru said, for she had called in there already, so she said, for cigarettes and some cigars.

"I know that, thanks," said Barbara.

"I'll keep you company," I said. "What will you do, Pru?"

So here we were, the three of us: me, since it seemed essential I should share in Barbara's plight. Or had I really come because I could not stand to wait alone when who knows who might come and tell me Maurice needed Clo? Nor could I bear to stand and listen while the wind got up and watch the TV weatherman put plastic storm clouds on the map of south-west England and the coast of northern France.

Pru claimed she came because if we were off round pubs and such, she wasn't going to miss the fun, and needed data from another pub besides the Lamb and Flag. She'd used that one in *Counterpunch*.

We got up speed and shot down Florence Avenue. "I think we should have left a note," I said.

To tell the truth I had had words with Joel. My smile was fixed. My banter in the car was only spume upon the surface of a seething sea, an underlying swell of fear, regret. Harsh words had passed between us late that afternoon. He came in, leaving Gerry in the car. He had his coat still on from work. "You're going out again?" I said.

I'd guessed that he would feel the need within the next few days to pit himself against some other evil or promote some other good. "You want me to stay in?" he said. He put his hands behind his back, began to pace the whole length of the room. I like the smell of Joel just home from work, the fresh

103

wood-shavings smell, the scent of linseed oil: "It would be nice," I said.

I hoped I could be delicate in my approach. I've always said I'd rather cut my throat than let him think I challenged him or gave him orders. "I only thought . . ."

"What did you think?" said Joel. Pru often comments on the way that men, who have been challenged in the way Joel was the night before, feel every face is turned against them now. "Now listen, darling heart . . ." he said.

"I'm sure you've things to do. I'll miss you though . . ."

"Old Gerry's in a state."

"He always is," I said. "Why don't you go to Whitley Bay?" I sat down at the table where I'd left my jewellery last night. We hadn't eaten at the table since. I wished I had said nothing about Whitley Bay.

"Why Whitley Bay? Why should I go to Whitley Bay? I hate to ask, my precious queen, but what is bugging you?"

"Well, nothing. Everything. All sorts of things. Things I haven't had a chance to talk about."

"Like what?" He, having stopped, began his pacing in his pale pink anorak, the one I chose for him last camping holiday.

My story was too long to tell. I put my bracelets on. I'm adult now, I thought. I'm grown up now. The job of woman is to deal with things and come up smiling when she's dealt, and so I spoke to him of trivialities. "For one—I've bought a garden frame. You didn't even know I'd bought a garden frame. At least I've ordered one . . . from Barbara . . . to cheer her up the other day."

"That's very nice of you, my sweet. It's typical of you to be considerate like that . . ."

I looked at him a little sharply then. He stood between me and the light. I could not accurately interpret his expression. "I am a little perfect on the whole," I said.

He sighed: "I knew it. Absolutely knew it. *That* was it. Last night. I didn't read from *Two in One* like I had said I would . . ."

"You shouldn't have. I mean I'm glad you didn't on the whole . . ."

"Oh yes! I've only fucked the whole week up."

"The idea that I'm perfect is proved false in any case . . . it follows that I can't be perfect if you have to go with Bruce for consolation . . ."

"So now it's Bruce!" he said.

"I don't mind Bruce at all. I like Bruce, actually. I like him being here. I only made the point that if I'm perfect, *I* would do . . . you could have talked with me and had a drink with me . . ."

"We will tell Bruce to leave. That's what we'll do."

That's typical, as Pru would say. Men think you want decisive action when you're only telling them what's wrong and what's too late to act upon. But then I made my worst mistake. I held a bracelet up and looked at him through that. A silly thing to do. It was a kind of wink maybe. It was a playful gesture, and an unwise one. I should have known suggestiveness was inappropriate. And also out of court. His pacing was a little faster now. He'd twigged the subtext of my gesture you might say.

You would think, wouldn't you, then, when there's man all open-necked and virile and there's woman, sitting there in need of him and knowing that if he would only bend his head a little way and let her put her arms around his soft warm neck that all would be resolvable.

Joel turned as sharply as if he'd put a warning finger out. I do remember thinking that there was a richness in the kind of subtlety between two people where a gesture which has not been made can be assumed: "Go on!" I said: "You want your orders to go out. I'm giving them."

"And how!"

"Go on! You want to go. Don't keep poor Gerry waiting any longer. As you so often say—in rootless situations of the kind in which we find ourselves we have to treat our friends as family and care for them . . ."

"I'll only go out if you want me to."

105

"All right. I'll lie and say I want you to."

"I think I'm going mad," he said.

"It's only when the contradiction gets too much to take we think we're going mad. It's rotten isn't it," I taunted him with all my silly expertise, "when something which you've claimed is perfect, i.e. woman, seems to be your natural enemy."

We haven't got a clock to tick or anything to pace the pauses out between us when we row, to raise the tension or to count the seconds as each one of us stands fraught with thoughts about the future and the past and frightened that we've reached a turning point. And ferns and variegated ivy, tradescantia and plants all round—if it is true they sense vibrations, wither with the beams of those, will need a lot of biograd to raise their heads and sprout out healthy leaves again.

This time he did put out his finger, wagged it, which he's never done before, and only did that I am sure because the pressure of the moment drove him to adopt the gestures of another man, a gesture which I've imitated often as a joke. "Now listen, clever clogs," he said. "Now listen very carefully. You should know now that no one ever patronises me, not ever . . ."

I also made a gesture that I've never made to him before, although I've made it in the past to . . . well to other men: I turned my back and tossed my head and said: "And if it's much too far to Whitley Bay, why don't you go down to the Ivy like you did last night? You can stay drinking there for hours and hours, and that will bring the wheel full circle, will it not? That's where we all came in . . ."

"That's where we all go out maybe," he said.

I wanted then to scream at him and tell him that he only said those words because they were a natural follow-on to what I've said and not because he meant that, darling heart.

So he had gone. It was as if he'd set out on a long crusade across the sea and had as final gesture stuck on me, as if I was an ancient trunk, the label 'Not Wanted on Voyage'.

With every word he'd spoken ringing in my ears, we women

sped along King Edward Road. We spoke of contradictions in the female role and future questions like, if men were now to be reduced to playthings, objects of desire, or almost children in a way, then could we castigate them for behaving in the manner of the role we offered them?

And in the Anchor off King Edward Road both Pru and I agreed that since pubs had been made by men, it didn't quite make sense for women to be using them to get away. And Barbara here took gin and tonic, me Campari, Pru a half of Tetleys and a whisky chaser. And in the Cheshire Arms right on the eastern fringe of town I said to Pru that in rejection of the role of angel in the hearth it might be hard to keep the fire alight. We had the same again and Barbara saw a man whom Ron played golf with sometimes and we had to stop her going up and telling him he'd spoilt her life.

We called in at the Packhorse Inn, repeated drinks, but after that we didn't stop for long in pubs. I said: "That's odd. I wonder if perhaps this kind of futile, functionless and effort-wasting, money-wasting trip . . . perhaps men feel like this. I mean, they *might* feel sort of lost. Perhaps they always feel like this, our sort of men, that is to say. Feel lost. For we are lucky in a way: there's always work at hand. We can improve the shining hour, are never at a loss, but they . . ."

"Not that old thing," said Pru. "No, that won't wash," and offered me a counter-argument I had not thought about. Convincing if I could remember it.

"Supposing they have come back by now," I said just after we had left the Packhorse Inn, "and Ron has started on the VAT. Perhaps we should . . ."

"Revenge is sweet," said Pru.

"Revenge is something men thought up," I said.

"Oh Christ," said Pru, who was beginning to feel queasy. She put her head down in her hands. "Oh Christ! Whichever way you look, you come right up against the whole thing being something they thought up, and even when you use the collective term 'they', you are not thinking of a group of living people, but a host of men through history . . ."

We were now aiming for a Country Club called Brick-worth, one which Barbara claimed Ron often visited and where there was a golf course probably. Pru found it on the map and said she'd guide us there. She'd love it, I was thinking, if they'd all been lured to golf with Ron. In fact she'd burst her sides with laughter at this thought. She'd relish the dramatic irony of their being forced into so bourgeois an activity.

We now were in the plain of York. The little car spun on amid expanse of fields, beneath high clouds which darkened further without giving rain. Land stretching out all sides of us, it was as if we were a tiny vessel on this sea of variegated greens and might go on for ever, on between these hedges, bridges, willows on the sides of rivers, villages we hardly noticed, duckponds, maypoles, grazing cows, the arch of sky from right to left, from north to south and east to west, a rainbow though there'd been no rain. Or could we drive and drive towards horizons so there might be no horizon in the end, or there might be the final one through which we'd cross and disappear?

I sat up, tried to shout in Pru's ear that, if all of us, if men and women drove like this like bats from hell to no good purpose and left no one watching angel-like in hearths, then who would dot the i's and cross the t's and make the teas and count the children in from school?

She may have heard, but all she shouted back was: "I'll put this in as peak for chapter twelve. She's driving off to meet the double-glazing man and has this glimpse of truth about the pointlessness of everything, and how in years and years she might just feel the bloke she's got is just about the same, all told, as the one she's passionate for getting. That would be so revolutionary in fiction of adultery. I mean, I don't think that it has been done. Correct me, but I could just do it, couldn't I?"

"But when in love, you know quite well," I shouted in her ear, "a woman doesn't think like that."

"Well, this one will," said Pru. "She will see everything in cosmic terms."

"But cosmic terms don't last," I yelled. "I mean you get a flash of cosmic thought and touch the meaning of the meaning and it's back to VAT and being with the man you *want* and not the man you don't, and that, if anything, is cosmic verity," I shouted vainly as we took a corner, Barbara, for the first time slowing down to look around at Pru for help because we'd reached a crossroads which said BRICKWORTH 2 on one arm of the sign and BRICKWORTH 3 miles on the other.

"That's too good to be true," said Pru.

I do remember thinking that the end of this would be a crash or even something slight like running out of petrol, and it would be men who came to help. I then remember thinking that, had any of us children under twelve or so, we would not be here, could not be here at this weird crossroads, immobile waiting where the road looked almost greeny black whichever way you looked. I thought: if woman is the same as woman was, and if we had fulfilled the pattern of our grandmothers, we would now be elderly because of all that nonstop giving birth. We would be sitting toothless on our hearths. Nor would there have been Lotuses Mark III perhaps to spin us off, and since the Lotus was designed by men, maybe there would have been no Lotus anyway. Which makes times out of joint again. We don't know which ideas to grasp. It must have been like this when people who had always held there was a structure which they thought divine and static, which was called the Chain of Being, which had angels at the top and things like mud and stones down at the bottom, began to have to change their minds and see all men as equal, vile but needing government. I shouted out all this to Pru.

"It isn't like it's been before," she shouted back. "Don't talk that shit."

I snapped. "O.K. then, *be* like that. But do you realise that it's all because of Gerry and the Grassington Award, him treating it as if it were the Nobel Prize!"

"You've got yourself confused there, dear. We're here because of Ron, the VAT, the silver wedding, Barbara's finer feelings . . . *and* I have to add, your fussing over Joel too much . . ."

"That isn't it. It's real for me. It's real for Barbara, too. O.K. for you! You'll get the people just the way you want them in the book, apportion pain in careful doses, be creative and improve on nature, so although for you this may be fiction, Pru, for us it's fact."

Now Pru was getting quite beside herself. She carried on about the narrow margins between fact and fiction and the character of Alan who, in *Counterpunch,* was only very loosely based on Gerry. And later on, in some brief pause when she had been behind a hedge (she has cystitis, so it seems) she let it be admitted that the scene in *Counterpunch* where Alan had a fuck with Gwyneth in the matrimonial bed was all lies anyway: "I ask you, Monica, can *you* see Gerry with his fear of being horsewhipped and all that, even coming *near* the house I lived in then?"

Which news would have been more of interest had I been in happy carefree frame of mind.

The Country Club was up a drive, mown grass at either side, a tarmacked track with laurels, rhododendrons, old iron fence and golf-green flags which stuck up in the rolling turf. Beside the fence a sign which read: '5 m.p.h. Watch Out. Children Playing'. I had to think of Joel again and the ice cream van outside the Ivy. Would we ever be together hand in hand and standing there?

A good expanse of car park, smooth. Men with golf clubs lifting them into the boots of cars. We drove through, swept around to check as we had checked throughout, for any of the cars we'd recognise. "Is that your Renault?" Barbara said to me.

"I can't remember what our number is," I said, quite suddenly.

"That isn't yours," said Barbara, and we drove away again.

Ron's yellow Volvo Estate: much later, darker in the market square.

The door into the Ivy is a faded blue, paint scratched and stained. The teenage disco had just shut down for the night. Large children like the ones who frightened Joel were scattering across the square, silently in running shoes.

A boy came up from lurking in the shadows. "You are the mother of Clarissa, yes?"

"She isn't here.'

"I must presume she has deserted Maurice Brett?"

"Oh yes. I *think* she has."

He was a smallish lad and dark-skinned as far as I could see. And as he moved into the pool of light shed by a dim lamp just above the Ivy door, I saw that he was Middle-Eastern looking, with short hair and limpid dark brown eyes: "I was just waiting. On the waiting list, it might be said." He pushed the door and held it open for me.

"Oh yes?" I said. "How many on the waiting list? She isn't here."

"Then I will wait."

"She won't be back for weeks."

We stood there in the small square lobby at the bottom of the stairs beside the gents, and people came downstairs and went in there and other people coming out, went up again. The echo of their voices came spasmodically, likewise did music from upstairs beyond the glass swing-door.

"I wait," the boy, whose age was difficult to guess, explained. "I must be early bird."

"She's not the worm," I said and made to go upstairs.

My mood was steely, unemotional by now. I could not be much moved by anything. I looked towards the boy. This was perhaps the Iraqi boy that Jamie spoke about, who was, so Jamie claimed, the son of someone powerful in Baghdad. He had himself, this lad, a military air, blue blazer with brass buttons on and highly polished shoes.

111

"1 know that when she comes, she will come to the Ivy first," he said.

I put my foot on to the bottom step: "But not, I think, if Maurice is in there."

"Are you suggesting that her love for him will have been replaced with something like repulsion?"

The stairs above me looked enormous. Each tread was very deep as if designed for giants, and from the puddle at the bottom of the stairs, there stretched a spattered stream of wetness, unidentifiable, I'm glad to say. Ron could not be in here, I thought, nor Gerry certainly, and if Joel was in here and had been in here last night what desperation would have driven him!

"Allow me to escort you up," I felt a light hand underneath my elbow.

"How kind." I picked my skirt up in one hand in order to begin the great ascent. From time to time I had to pause for breath, while he stood there beside me, slightly bowed, his hands behind his back. Then, when I made to take a further step, he took my arm again. I felt quite sorry I had been so short with him and made some efforts at initiating conversation on any topic which did not touch on Clo. He smelt of sandalwood or something very clean. I tried to think of what I'd heard in recent weeks about Iraq. Perhaps it was an earthquake or an army coup. Or was it that a general had been deposed? I could not quite remember so I said: "How are things in Iraq?"

"I hope to have a most important part to play at home," he said. "I am here to study health, preventive medicine, drains in depths, diseases that you get from them . . . when I have finished learning English well." He rested one leg on the step above, knee bent and trouser leg now lifted to reveal a creamy white silk sock.

"You speak it very well already. It's remarkable," I said.

"How kind of you." We paused again. I leaned against the cold stone wall. The swing-door at the top was open and a denimed figure, bearded and bow-legged stood there, then

lurched on down towards us, hurtled, you might say, gorilla-
like. The Arab boy moved back to let him pass.

We struggled on. His name was Hamid, so he said. He
went on talking of Iraq. "I speak of bad diseases, but
my parents have a large grand house in the suburbs of
Baghdad . . ."

"So things are prospering," I said.

He turned and looked me in the eyes, speaking almost
fiercely. "For a people that has lived in feudal servitude for
centuries, how can that be?" I hoped he would not desert
me now. The Ivy is a club. I might need signing in. "But all
the same," he added in a softer voice, "it is the case that if
Clarissa came to live there, she would have a home of luxury."
I could not help but feel a touch of pride that Clo had been
considered fit for such a destiny. I saw her lying back on
silken cushions, wearing see-through baggy trousers and with
handmaidens kneeling offering delights. "And a life of purpose helping with the people's struggle," Hamid added and
I changed my image, seeing Clo in boots and khaki,
shouldering a rifle in the desert.

We'd reached the top, surmounted all those steps. The
sound of music had grown louder and the swing-doors moved.
Perhaps the wind again.

"We shall not hear to speak in there," he said, "so may I
say right now, I think Clarissa very beautiful, and if you've
heard about the girl I keep in Leeds, I can assure you that
is quite unmeaningful . . ."

I looked back down the stairs, the puddled treads. A smell
of disinfectant wafted up. "Shall we go in?" I said. The
smell was mixed with that of beer and urine. I felt inside
my bag and found a rather crumpled Kleenex which I held
up to my nose. The Iraqi stood and looked at me in the
eye. "I think Clarissa is in there. You're looking for Clarissa,"
he seemed to be accusing me. He held his head straight up.
His collar was extremely white and crisp, his shoulders
straight. There was a competence about him, whether for
preventive medicine or the struggle of the people.

"Clo is not here," I said, "I'm going in to ... to meet my husband actually, and the husband of a friend ... well several men, I think."

I'd left them, Pru and Barbara, in the market square, the Lotus parked beside the Volvo which was parked in turn beside King Edward's statue. Not many buildings in the square had lights still on. "We don't know if they're all together anyway," I said. We had tried ringing all three houses several times. "Of course they might have all gone home," I said, "and all have gone to bed. Joel doesn't hear the phone upstairs, and Gerry might have had his earphones on."

"And doing VAT makes people deaf, I've heard," said Barbara, who had mostly lapsed into a brooding silence by this time.

"If it's just Ron," said Pru. She looked around the square. "He might have gone into Lloyds Bank. I *know* it's shut. Of course I know it's shut, but managers do live over banks I think sometimes. Supposing Ron had gone in for a VAT consultation ..." Pru's main intention was, I guessed, to go home, get to bed, or maybe to write up impressions of the hectic drive for *See-Through Man*.

Barbara drummed her fingers on the steering wheel: "We bank at National Westminster," she said.

"I would go in there to the Ivy, Barbara, if you wanted that," I said. She didn't answer, so I touched her on the shoulder.

"You do whatever you think's best." Her voice was spiritless and had no timbre.

Pru looked around the square again. "Electricity show-rooms?"

"Look," I said, "if you are bored of looking, Pru, go home. I'll go in there. Or if you want to, you go in, but one of us must stay with Barbara ..."

"You go then, dear," said Pru, "like Barbara says, you do what you think's best ..."

114

Hamid leaned one hand and pushed the swing-door open, and the Ivy seemed a much less likely place than even I had thought. I felt the music through my feet as well as through my ears. And backs to me a crowd of people and ahead a stage with banks of sound equipment on. The bar was to the right. A noise as deafening as any seagull horde. The Iraqi nodded, smiling, talking still. I nodded back. How much of life, I mused, is spent in talking over noise. Or talking over silence, when you come to think of it. He seemed to indicate he would not like to leave me standing here beside the door, and that he'd like to get a drink for me. I tried to yell at him I thought that Arabs didn't drink; then wondered if I'd got that wrong. All Iraqis, after all, may not be Arabs, though with a name like Hamid surely ... oh well, never mind. Was that a glimpse of Bruce, blond hair, a floppy fringe, now shaken back?

The people here were mostly Maurice-like, not young, not old, not clean, not dirty on the whole, although the lights were low and smoke hung in the air above their heads. The Iraqi boy came back and carried in each hand a drink. He offered me the glass of greenish stuff. I smiled and wondered what I'd said that made him think I'd asked for Crème de Menthe. I had to raise my voice and ask him if he'd hold my drink a little longer for me, since I had to go and find my husband and his friend and yet another friend, but I would be right back. He leaned towards me, mouthing still. I think he said: "They have a lot of stabbings here. Be careful, please."

I aimed for Bruce, but first I looked around. And was that Zoe who had come that afternoon? And was that Sylvia? My eardrums seemed to fill with thudding fluff. The room that still is pink but faded, greyish pink, with lowish ceilings seemed to burst with all that noise, and ringing tones which seemed to come from a loudspeaker near my head, but might have had their source inside my head. I pressed on, turning shoulders, this way, that way, sideways through the crowd. At least if I could reach Bruce anyway.

A hand made contact with my back. I turned, looked up. Big Paul, who lives two doors from us and goes around with Ashley quite a bit. "Heyup!" he seemed to say to me. He gestured with his head to where I had left Hamid standing with the drinks.

Big Paul is six foot five or six at least. I could not reach to shout into his ear. In any case I am not drawn to him. He has a kind of jeering cockiness which makes me feel uneasy, and he stands half naked in a window of his mother's house all times of year, as if to show the passers-by the wealth of hair upon his chest. "You taken over now?" He was referring to Hamid again, I think.

"No, not at all," I tried to shout. "Have you seen Ron?"

"He is a prince, they say, that one! You could do worse."

He went away, a glass of beer above his head, the giant perhaps for whom those stairs had been designed. And I was stuck and could not follow in his wake, nor did I wish to anyhow. Hemmed in, I was, on every side. Beside me bodies and above me smoke, and through that smoke the ceiling with its stains and cracks, a network of fine hair-sized cracks, and if they'd seemed before my eyes to widen out I could not speak or call for help or shout out warnings or send up maroons that this, this edifice was soon to crumble underneath the pressure of the feet, which feet would not have sensed potential tremors from below. And if it fell, the cracked-up bricks and mortar, floorboards, joists and plaster pillars would just heave into the square, and heads of mousy unwashed hair would poke up, denimed arms would writhe and fingers twitch for helping hands.

A rough sea this, like being deep down in a trough between two waves, not seeing other ships behind the crests of other waves, except the tallest ships. My foot was trodden on. If Joel is here, I thought, I'll only just forgive him since he claims this is an evil place, but it is nothing but a place which might fall down, a place you get your feet stepped on and lose one shoe. And then I thought, if only Joel were here I would forgive him anything, and bent to put my shoe

116

back on. Down there, deep in the sea of worn down Wrangler shoes, Doc Martins boots all scuffed, I put my high-heeled sandal on again and felt that if I stayed down there, I would be left unnoticed till a cleaner (if they have one) found me crouched there in the morning. But Joel was wrong, I thought, there's nothing here but people having smelly feet and they outnumber us. Remember what Pru said about the birthrate 1959. Remember there are more of them than us, and more means worse, you say, and lotus eating must be shared and lotuses are limited, cannot go round and lotuses are made by men. And when this lot are old, the crowded places will be old folk's homes and there they'll sit in cardigans in double and in treble rows in windows looking out, if there is any place can hold them all.

A group of dancers in the middle of the room. My ears by now accustomed to the noise. And then the lights were lowered and the beat came through, a thumping tune I'd heard before. One word of it—perhaps the only word I caught —was 'tiger' and the whole evoked in me the feel of jungle drums, was loud and not entirely irresistible. I could have stood there rooted to the spot and swayed. And in the tiny space I occupied I felt like dancing on my own, began to make a lunging movement, lifted up my feet and even stamped. It didn't matter who stood next to me and moved in common rhythm, but I felt the need to swing my hips and raise my arms above my head. All thoughts shut off, I was anonymous in darkness, could not be seen except when strobe lights flashed. I stamped but could not hear my wooden sandals meet the floor. The people who'd been mousy-haired in smoky light before were suddenly revealed as black and white and brilliant violet. They tossed their heads, their hair flew up. They were possessors now of grace and dignity. And this was good, not evil any of it. Oh Joel, I'd love to dance with you again. And, if my eardrums split, my eardrums split, because I am a throbbing, stamping, war-like African and then a jogging, hopping, bouncing doll and then a sailor hornpiping, and when the music calls for it a leaping lord. If there was

117

room I'd arabesque. I was the generation of the jitterbug and can do that as well.

The lights went on. My eyes were lifted to the goal of Bruce again. About this time his head moved out of sight and then moved back again, a rocking jerking movement. Maybe he was laughing, rocking on his feet. He sometimes does. The heads around him moved as well, went down, came up again, and people who had ducked, stayed ducked. One boy who looked a bit like Maurice, but with thicker hair on top, came on towards me on his knees, another seemed to lean away towards the wall and crumpled out of sight. I'd danced but now stood still. The movement was outside me, not within. I even heard a shout above the music, and my feet were wet, likewise my back. Some beer had spilt. Or what had spilt? I looked down at my shoes but could not see them any more. Someone on the floor was crawling there across my feet. Her skirt impeded her. I crawled across Pru's border just like that on Sunday, was it Sunday, skirt impeding me?

This was another fracas at the Ivy. They have them often so I read and hear, policemen waiting in the square to pick the culprits up, policemen knowing this is where the trouble is most likely to break out, that this is where arrests are to be made, policemen knowing, sensibly for all I know, that what with yin and yang and one thing and another, it might as well be here as anywhere. I turned to leave.

Behind me pressure of a hundred backs. Like crushes in the London Underground where people fall beneath the feet of others and are crushed, or of films of football stadiums where barriers give way.

Not everyone it seemed was pushing to get out like me. A tall boy, pimple-faced in checked sweater stood his ground. He had just let me through and did not wish to shift his feet again. I wedged one arm between him and his next-door neighbour, then my other arm and dived between them and was caught against another solid wall of bodies there. The Iraqi boy was now in view, still standing with the drinks

118

in hand. I reached him, turned and saw Bruce was being dragged between two other lads, supported and with bleeding face.

The door swung open. I went through. Then Hamid came. The boys with Bruce in tow came next and put him down beside a hatstand. There he sat, his head now swathed with greasy anoraks. I looked around at all of them as if to say what do we do now please? The boys had left. They ran. But half way down the stairs they slowed and walked with swaggeringly casual steps as if they were about to leave by choice. At any rate they swiftly disappeared.

Blood trickled down the left side of Bruce's face, a narrow winding stream of it. I offered him a crumpled Kleenex which he held to it, then tried to stand, but had to sit, fell back, his head between his knees. Beside me now was Hamid, saying: "That looks a very nasty bash or cut indeed. It will need stitches. We will take him to the hospital in my car, but first we must assist him down the stairs. Oh, by the way, I take it that this *is* a friend of yours?"

"You could say that," I said. Then turned to Bruce. "Who *did* that, Bruce?"

"That fucking Maurice fucking Brett."

A long way down to go, like cliffs, like setting off to see the lifeboat come out of its shed with pluming curl of crest of wave, two pluming curls of crest of waves and I had thought that girls like Clo could flit from flower to flower if one can call them flowers. "No. Most unwise. He might need anaesthetic for the stitches." This boy's no fool, I thought, a prince maybe but not a fool.

He drank his babycham. "We cannot get this in Iraq," he said and put both glasses down behind the hatstand, hidden.

"You have a car?" I said.

"A large car, yes, but first we take it slowly down the stairs. We must look like the three of us are leaving by desire and not by force," he said, "or otherwise we will be noticed by police. My father would be most upset." He leaned down, put a hand to Bruce, began to hitch him to his feet. "Well, fuck your Dad," said Bruce. I took the other side and wished that Bruce had not said that.

"This *is* a friend of yours?" said Hamid. I noticed that he had a downy small and very black moustache. His eyes were sharp—not limpid now.

I had to go in front. Hamid took the weight of Bruce upon the left, and Bruce put down his right arm, clutched my shoulder while I in turn was much involved with clutching up my skirt and wobbled on my high-heeled shoes. I paused: "Hang on. Look! Wait!" I took my shoes off, threw them down in front of me. They clattered, bounced on every other tread and landed on the concrete by the door. And now my feet were on the cold but sticky steps. I felt whatever had been spilt oozing between my toes. "You should not have done that," said Hamid about the shoes. "It will attract attention even more."

The weight of Bruce was more than I'd expected and I had to watch each step in case I faltered. And at every step I feared that one of Hamid's leather shoes would come down on my toes, and that might well dislodge me as I tried to get my balance right. I felt warm trickles on my neck and this was Bruce's blood which must have reached his chin and then his neck and run down that inside his shirt and on to me, and then on to my shirt and down inside my sleeve. We stood and rested half way down: "Did you say Maurice, Bruce?" I asked, because at least that meant that Maurice was alive and well and reasonably strong. But later on I wished I had not asked that question at that time.

"Oh fuck I don't know," Bruce said weakly, "and I'm sorry for the blood."

"Well, shall we go on now?" I looked at Hamid. He stood there, gazing out ahead, but still held Bruce around the waist. I had just put a foot out cautiously to take the next tread down. I drew it back and waited like a dancer in mid-hop. It wasn't easy and I had to try hard not to let my weight fall back against the two of theirs. "Well, on we go?" I said.

Hamid seemed rooted to the spot. He turned to Bruce, and

in his eyes was all the flash of Middle-Eastern trouble spots. He had a definitely burning look, the kind of look Joel gets when he sees commercials which exploit, the kind of look Joel shot me down with when he said I must not patronise and turned upon his heel and left. A draught of air came up towards us from the open door on to the street. A strongish draught, it must have been. My skirt, though damp with stickiness and heavy round the hem, was lifted up. The door banged on its hinges, echoed up. I felt Bruce heavier on me. Had Hamid's grip slackened then? And were we now to plunge the twelve or so remaining steps and crash in head-long skull-shattering collapse the three of us? Hamid looked transfixed. Head sharply turned, chin up, he looked at Bruce: "Have you had carnal knowledge of Clarissa, then?"

To say I did not know exactly what to do is greatly to understate the situation. There were so many moral threads caught up in it. Dynamic threads as well. For if I acted, it might topple us. I chose the moral threads. I had to speak. And then I had to find the words. And if I didn't find the words . . .

What would Joel do? And in the asking of that question, it's implicit that I think of Joel when moral issues are in question. Which proved to me that at the screaming point in time, I needed him and could not act without him or the knowledge of his deep committal to my cause. And if I'd fallen, toppled and cascaded down those steps and cracked my skull and lain there crumpled awkwardly with one arm bent beneath my spine and one leg splayed as people do in films, my last words would be "Joel!" and "Joel!" and not much else in way of final words.

But that's in retrospect. The moment called for instant action. There are not a lot of moments in a life like this perhaps. It's called the crunch, the testing time and some take an heroic path at crunches, some do not . . . Well, anyway . . . Dynamics now dictated and I had to speak. I swear I had to speak. I had to think of something which could not be argued, plead the case for Bruce's innocence to Hamid, indisputably. And now, in further retrospect, the retrospect of days, I've thought of several other things I could have said. I could have said that Bruce and Maurice were long-standing enemies, that Bruce was championing Clo to save her for deserving lovers—like Hamid himself. Or that Maurice was a boy of violent nature. The wind was fanning in my face and lifting up my hair. It seemed to blast against us all and push us back, was cold, as cold as concrete was beneath my wet bruised feet. I turned to Hamid: "I think you should not speak like that. It is my daughter you are speaking of. This young man, Bruce, I mean, has not had carnal knowledge of my daughter ever. Apart from anything . . ." and here I hestitated because I saw his eyes glow more, and when I turned to look downstairs I saw both Pru and Barbara standing there; their coats, one white, one black, were blowing round their legs, and I went on: "Apart from anything, he is not capable of things like that. He has had trouble of that kind for many years. You should extend your sympathy, I think, to this poor boy . . ."

Oh Joel, I've thought of such a lot of things I might have said, so many other words, so many other points I could have made, so many other cases and defences, Joel. I'll make it up to Bruce and you and Gerry, Ron as well and Ashley, Jamie, even James.

I reached a hand to Pru when getting to the bottom step. She handed me my shoes. "They were not there," I said, "I mean the men."

The casualty waiting-room is long and low, an annexe, airport-like. The chairs for those who wait are plastic, orange-backed, arranged along the side. The floor is charcoal grey ribbed rubber tiles, and wheelchairs, stretchers, run on these without a sound. We sat, the three of us, while Bruce was wheeled away into a cubicle. The sister, small, red-haired and Irish said: "He won't be long."

We'd squeezed Bruce into Barbara's car. Blood oozed out on to leather seats and Barbara put a Kleenex to the wound. Hamid stood by a streetlight watching, puzzled possibly, then got into his Volvo Estate and drove away. To put the record straight, this small mistake of Barbara's which concerned one digit on the registration plate, is the only factual error I have ever known her make. In every other detail, Hamid's car was identical to Ron's.

Pru's hat was on her knee. She borrowed Barbara's comb and tried to comb her knotted corkscrew curls and then gave up. Barbara's hair was neat and sprung in little highlit waves around her head. She'd taken off her long silk scarf and wrapped it round her hands, it seemed in tension of a kind. We hardly spoke.

The end door opened. Terence Meadowcroft, the doctor, hurried through with leather bag. His old tweed suit, the one he comes to poetry readings in, his grey hair thick, a boy's hair with a fringe. He's bowed at shoulders, possibly from living with Suzy Meadowcroft. The thought of her reminded me of Joel last night.

Pru said: "I'm going out to have a smoke," and disappeared for quite some time.

The door again. We all looked up. I half expected Hamid to come in search of Bruce again. I more than half hoped Joel would come. How could he know that we were here?

But this was neither Hamid nor yet Joel. It was a girl, a very pretty girl. In uniform, white shirt, black tie, thin black legs in stockings which had seams. Her shoes were polished. A WPC I often have admired in town. A girl, I'm told, who throws the javelin for Yorkshire and who nearly made the Olympic team for Montreal.

But Barbara flinched. Not from any racial prejudice I'm sure but rather since she sees police like Vatmen as her natural enemies. Meanwhile the WPC's presence made me wonder if we should inform on Maurice, have him put into a cell away from all potential overdoses for at least one night. Her presence also made me wonder if it could not be that Clo might one day wear a uniform like that? With springing step, as if about to run and launch her javelin, the WPC walked up and down in front of us. Then Bruce cried out in pain as stitches were put in.

123

I wore a uniform just once, the time Bruce made a film of us. A touch Polanskiesque perhaps, a little violent and surrealist. He needed someone to be dressed up as a woman in the forces, and I dressed as WRNS first officer, with braid around my cuffs. I have to say I never felt so purposeful, correctly dressed and with a sense of being in control of things. And Joel, as well, a tank corps colonel which is what he should have been but born too late alas.

Then Terence Meadowcroft came out with bag. He didn't seem to see me there, but I was curled up with my arms wrapped round myself against a creeping cold which did not stem from air around because the waiting place was heated with a kind of blowing fan of heat, the rhythmic throb of which was like a heartbeat all around, cocooning us.

The doctor stopped and spoke, but not to us: "All well," I heard him say or rather ask: "No trouble, WPC Le Mesurier?"

"No, everything is fine tonight," she said in lilting tone.

He nodded at the cubicle, from which Bruce had not yet appeared. "Another Ivy bash."

She raised her eyebrows: "Oh, has there been? I will report." She took her walkie-talkie set, unhooked it from the pocket of her shirt.

"Not bad. Not bad," said Terence, strolling with her to the door, his bag in hand. This banged against his baggy trousers as he limped along (he has a war wound from Korea), while she with swinging hips stepped lightly at his side.

I leaned a little forward, was about to rise, but Barbara held me there and whispered: "Don't do owt. Do nowt. Just sit."

"There's nothing they can do to us," I whispered back.

"Don't get involved."

Terence Meadowcroft had gone by now and WPC Le Mesurier hovered in the centre of the open space and then approached the cubicle. Why did I try to stop her? I have thought of this and still don't know. Perhaps it was for Bruce's sake. He'd had enough: the wound from Maurice, then my wounding words. Why did I wrench myself from

124

Barbara's grip upon my skirt and run across and say that if Bruce must be questioned, so must I. I was a witness after all. I cleared my throat: "I am responsible for him," I said. "He may be over twenty-one, but he is in my care ... I do not want him questioned now."

Then Bruce was pushed out as the curtains were drawn back and lay there on the stretcher looking up at us. The cut was stitched and plastered up. A swelling and discoloured bruise surrounded it; dried blood was on his forehead, cheek and chin. The sister helped him off the stretcher, sat him down a little way from Barbara. She dusted him a little, dabbed him with a piece of lint she held and said: "Well, there you are! Well, there you are, my son! Is that your Mummy there? Oh look! There's Daddy too."

I hadn't seen Joel come. The sister said: "Or maybe it was Daddy did it? Daddy getting stroppy eh?" Her voice, I must presume, was teasing and facetious.

It is possibly of interest that I discovered as the evening wore on from one crisis to the next, that I found the need to speak more forcefully and yet again more stridently and almost raucously, but clearly with commanding voice as if I too wore uniform again. Although I was, to say the least, in a bedraggled state. My skirt was stained with beer and Bruce's blood, my shirt as well. I'd left one shoe in Barbara's car because it was too sticky and disgusting. The foot that it had been upon was grey with clinging dust from where I'd walked with Bruce into the hospital. I must have been lopsided too.

"This man," I gestured with my hand to Joel, "is not the father of this boy." Both nurse and policewoman raised their eyebrows at this point. "He's not the father of this boy and he has never, to my knowledge, struck a blow in anger in his life."

"This time I did," said Joel.

I gazed at him with open mouth. "You weren't there at the ..." but just in time I felt the pressure of Joel's Hush Puppy on my own bare foot. Suede shoe it may have been,

125

but then my feet were tender and it hurt. I winced, but took the hint.

WPC Le Mesurier had taken out her notepad and her walkie-talkie she was holding still. Joel smiled down at her. He smiled as warmly and as charmingly as ever he has smiled at anyone, even at Doreen Savory the time he lay beside her in the king-size bed the other night, and me at any time for what seems months. He held my arm and drew me close towards him, held me by his side. She put the walkie-talkie back a little slowly, still looking up into Joel's eyes. Perhaps, like me, she'll look into Joel's eyes and nothing ever will be quite the same again. She could not get the walkie-talkie hooked exactly in the tab above her breast. Joel could not take his eyes off her. Or did not take his eyes off her.

Notebook in hand, she licked her lips and took her pen out of her other, right breast pocket. She said: "I'll call it a domestic then. No further action needed."

Domestic, yes. Would Joel and I now have our own domestic? Bruce was in his bed, his face turned to the wall, and Pru and Gerry had gone home. A silence from next door, and Joel and I sat back to back. Our big brass bed was strewn with metaphoric broken glass, the kind of broken glass I'd crawl across for him.

There is a verse in *Two in One*. A tree, the man and woman either side of it. They wait for fruit to fall, un-Eden like, but never touch or shake a branch. The final line: 'No questions asked.'

I mustered some endearments in my mind. I would have reached for the Thesaurus had I dared to break the spell. I needed words, words better than the ones which came to mind which were along the lines of: 'Sweetest, light of my life, you came to rescue me. Oh brave new world . . .' But somehow when you have been over clever, being over canny doesn't work too well.

Joel lay across the bed still dressed. His eyes were closed. I searched for eyelid movement, flutterings. No questions asked however, even: was sleep feigned?

126

Friday: a.m.

Perhaps if these, my memoirs, ever see the light of press
there will be questions asked like (a) but where was Ron?
(b) what were the others doing? and (c) how did Joel know
where to find us? The only one I know an answer to is (a),
and Ron was playing golf (with Bruce and Ashley as it happens). At ten he went home, did the VAT and didn't for
some reason answer the telephone. A footnote only this.

Another footnote: I started out to write about our life and
art—to show us all at work, creatively. That hasn't happened
much, although I will just mention that on Friday usually I
work on haikus or translating Horace, something of that kind.
This Friday though I planned to write a Silver Wedding Ode
for Ron and Barbara. I'd got a list of words to rhyme with
Ron—like 'gone' and 'marathon' and many more appropriate
than that. As far as Barbara was concerned, I reckoned
'harbour' (safe) might be the poem's *tour de force*.

However, nothing came of that.

"Is everything all right?" said Clo. She'd rung to say they
were about to sail.

"Yes, fine."

"Your voice sounds funny."

"I am perfectly all right."

This time the gulls were quiet, although I thought I heard
the roar of wind, or maybe it was waves on rocks below the
cliff. Perhaps I should have asked what happened to the lifeboat when it went out on the last occasion that she rang.

"You will come back?" I said.

"Your voice *is* odd. Is Jamie coming on his own?"

"I'll see to that."

She said: "I've written to you, told you everything . . ."

"Oh thanks . . . what everything?"

The call was over and I had not asked her how the weather was. But here was hot—that anticyclone over Jutland strengthening it seemed. Deciding I would go and buy a silver wedding present after all, I set off into town and drove recalling all the things I should have said to Clo, including that she must ring up the moment that she got the other side, and how much money did she have and was she really going to hitch there all that way?

Before I left the house Bruce had come down. He sat there in the garden. "All right, Bruce?"

He looked away.

"How's Harry head?" I asked again.

He'd taken my dark glasses to disguise his cut and bruise. He sat there on our canvas chair in shorts and shirt.

"Hey, Bruce?"

In town the streets were only bearable to walk in on the shady side. And people sat relaxed beneath the red umbrellas of the Café des Chevaux. If you closed your eyes, half closed them to exclude on either side the Post Office and the Chinese Take Away, you might just be in France. But thoughts of France disturbed me, and I stood there, blankly, while the bus which comes from Leeds swept down into the square and circled round. I stood there trying to remember what I'd come to town to do and felt the bus's heat and diesel smell.

I delved deep into my capacious bag to find my shopping list. The sun was on my back and beating through my shirt. My straw hat was but weak protection to my head. The glare distorted sight, and as I looked down far into my bag, its contents faded to a blur of papers, Kleenex, small change and spilt pills of different kinds. The letter I withdrew, believing it to be my shopping list, was one I'd had from Clo some days ago, and, sticking to its paste upon its envelope was the postcard Jamie sent. I panicked, delved again, and soon was picking tickets for the library, a cleaner's counterfoil for one of Joel's suits I have not yet collected, combs and bills, and

128

these were welling up and spilling on the pavement. Assorted pills were scattered at my feet. I could not tell what kind they were. I knelt. My hat fell off. I picked it up and used it as a basket, filling it with all the bits which constitute the sordid minutiae of my life.

I am governed by the stuff I use, I thought, and nearly wept as people on this busy day swept past, and some were crushing valium pills or maybe they were vitamins, with sandalled feet, ignoring my confusion and distress. Until a shadow fell across the scattered mess, a long tall shadow on the patch where I was bending down and hatless. I struggled to my feet. My hands were filthy from the pavement and I wiped them on my skirt. Shading my eyes I looked into a face and saw it was Theresa, Bruce's friend.

I could not quite decide if I was pleased or not to see her. I almost had forgotten her, to tell the truth, forgotten her existence, and I tipped the bits and pieces from my hat into my bag. "I know," I said to play for time, "why don't we have a drink?" She followed me across the square.

We weaved our way between parked cars, and near the cars the heat reflected from them hit us with metallic force. I felt quite faint and was obliged to take my hat off once again and fan myself.

She must have come for Bruce. Perhaps it would be better if he went with her. I had to think. At the Café des Chevaux there was one table spare. I noticed faces from last night but sat as if I had not seen them there. Theresa took a metal chair and sat on it and I sat opposite. She wore a T-shirt with a phallic symbol on the front and jeans which had been sawn off at the knee. Her eye make-up and frizzy Afro hair gave her a formidable look.

"So have you come out on the bus?" I said.

We both had milkshakes. Mine was raspberry. Hers was chocolate. Synthetic raspberry is the one concocted flavour I can bear. In fact I rather like it. Café des Chevaux makes milkshakes out of ice cream and real cream and so they have a creaminess you don't get everywhere. It's nice to sit there outside on a summer day and hear them whizzing up more shakes inside.

"Where's Bruce? He hasn't been to college, not for days," Theresa said. She is a big round girl with dimpled elbows. I kept on thinking just how fit she looked. "Ah, Bruce!" I said and sucked my milkshake straw and felt the coolness and the smooth consistency.

The heat intensified as yet another bus from Leeds came down into the square and puffed hot diesel fumes across the pavement. Then a rush of people pushing past our chairs. I saw Theresa for a minute as through a filtered lens and saw her as a preying girl; her prey was Bruce. Her ruddy beefiness, his wounded whiteness in the sun. Theresa in pursuit. I poked around inside my bag in case the shopping list had turned up somewhere in the mêlée.

She had been talking for some time. I hadn't listened very hard, but said from time to time: "Bruce really isn't ready yet to settle down. Theresa dear," and flicked a wasp away and thought that it was early in the year for wasps. Heat shimmered in the roadway or it may have been the diesel fumes. In case it was the diesel fumes I kept on watching, since I've always doubted that we could have heat that shimmered here.

"I'm through with him," Theresa said.

I looked up sharply: "Through with him?"

"Yes, through with him. I'm through with college too and all that art and stuff. My Mum and Dad are paying for a typing course . . ."

"I'm sure that will be very useful, but . . ." I found a folded paper, which I took, unfolded, spread upon the red enamel table. Not my shopping list but something which I must have picked up by mistake. It had Joel's writing on it. "That's very sensible"—I went on speaking to Theresa—"I mean, you never know—he might have gone back to Australia, then where would you be?"

Joel's writing was a poem with the title 'Breaking Point'. Theresa went on saying that she realised now her Mum was right, that Bruce was foreign and he did not know our ways. No doubt I should have argued with her, racist girl. Instead I puzzled over Joel's few lines:

They fatten there, injected with an agent,
Where once we turned the soil with heavy spade,
We stay as passive marrow now,
Dog-like, and not devoted, but devoured.
Nor passionless.
The war is on. No guns alas
With which to hammer home.
And so we fight away today.

It was an angry poem. Less well structured than his usual work, but possibly the angriest thing he's written for some years.

Theresa leaned back from the table, swung her large long legs and lit a Gauloises cigarette. She spoke about the typing course her mother had suggested she should do, what secretaries earned, how she would have a car quite soon and choose her men, not wait for them. Distracted as I was by the contents of Joel's poem, I could see her confidence was brittle and skin deep. But did he really see himself as passive marrow while I took up the syringe and brandished it, injected him? And had he wanted me to read these lines?

Theresa reached into the pocket of her jeans, produced an envelope and put it on the table just in front of me. "You've written Bruce a letter?" and I looked across the square and saw that where I'd spilt the contents of my bag not half an hour ago, a woman bent and picked a small thing off the ground.

"You give it him," Theresa said.

"Of course I will." I rose and picked my bag up, wondered if I should shake hands with her.

"It's what they gave me at the clinic," said Theresa, standing up as well, her hands stuffed in the pockets of her jeans, although the pockets were already stretched as tight as possible across her bottom. I marvel sometimes at the strength of

131

denim. As I took the envelope, I saw her in an office with a so-called boss across the desk, but one who cringed.

"The clinic? You've been ill?" I said.

"You give him that. He has to fill in where he's been and send it back. And tell him not to put it anywhere until he's clear."

"Put this?" I held the envelope.

"Not that."

I nodded. Slowly things were falling into place. She swaggered off, her bright red sandals laced around strong calves. She turned and said: "Your Clo will know. Your Clo will understand."

She went and waited by the bus stop and I saw her watching me across the square. I stood beneath King Edward's statue for a moment. I thought of shopping, but such was her presence there across the road from me, I felt obliged to get into the car and drive on home to give the envelope to Bruce without delay.

Dire calculations filled my mind. I don't remember driving home, but must have passed the Bingo Hall, the Supermarket and gone through all the Mavises and Muriels, the Phyllises and Florences, and thought that though I'm glad I was not born as long ago as people who were given names like that, such people did not have the problems poor Theresa has. If anyone held guns, the way Joel mentioned in his verse, it would most surely be Theresa, a machine-gun. She would stand there underneath King Edward, firing and not always over people's heads, a member of the Yorkshire Baader Meinhof branch.

The canvas chair was empty. Then I heard the phone ring. No one here but me to answer it.

I drove off straight away again. The call had been from Jamie.

"But you don't come home until tomorrow . . ."

"Here I am."

"The camp ends Saturday."

"I am at Skipton station. There was no connection."

I ran upstairs and searched through piles of paper on my desk to find the brochure with the picture of the camp, the bright mown grass, the pine trees sloping to the lake, log cabins. "You were very lucky that I had the car today," I said.

It wasn't until some time after leaving Skipton station that I realised that I had not kissed him as I would have had he come tomorrow, as I'm sure was planned. I could not find the brochure on my desk. "It was today," he said.

The scenery looked unfamiliar, the hedges hazed. I then remembered that I'd left my glasses on the table at the Café des Chevaux. We were up on high ground now and looking down on fields and lush grass valleys where sheep grazed. "And did you have a lovely time?" I said.

At least he'd picked his rucksack up himself and slung it in the boot. He looked the same, was neither browner nor yet thinner, just marginally a different shade. "It was O.K.," he said.

"Well, there you are."

I took the turn out of the station yard and through the town where it would seem it was a market day. Striped awnings dazzled me.

"It wasn't *that* O.K.," he said.

His hair was dry, uncombed, not neat and flat as usual. A badge was on his tracksuit top, and as a rule he doesn't put on badges, thinks they show too much committal or are showing off.

"You got a badge at any rate," I said. "At least you won a badge."

"I didn't win it. I just got the badge."

"What does it say?"

At least with Jamie you can drive for hours in silence and pursue your own reflections while he sits. Until you stop and wonder what his own reflections are and know that you will never in a hundred years find out.

"What does it say, the badge?" I said.

"It's got a number on it," Jamie said. "It's twenty-five."

133

He took a Mars bar from his pocket, bit a chunk off it and offered it to me to have another bite. I shook my head. "You did the twenty-five-mile walk?"

Some pylons crossed the fields ahead of us and climbed a hill. The cables disappeared beyond the rounded top and traffic, caravans as well as cars and trucks, was pouring in the opposite direction—to the Dales, because this was about to be the weekend.

"I didn't do the twenty-five-mile walk."

"You didn't do the twenty-five-mile walk?"

He picked the paper up, the *Guardian* I'd bought in town, the only thing I'd bought. "It says here," Jamie said, "that Russian tanks could sweep across the whole of Western Europe in three days."

"I thought they checked you on those walks," I said.

"It also says . . . they're bouncing laser beams off satellites."

"I thought they checked you on those walks, I said just now."

"The man who did the checking was away that day."

We slowed down where some traffic lights had been installed by workmen on the road. A feature I did not remember passing on the way, although I had been deep in thought. 'WAIT HERE WHILE GREEN LIGHT OPPERATES' the notice said.

'What did you do?" I said to Jamie as I braked to stop.

"I caught a bus."

The light in front of us turned green.

"Go on!" said Jamie.

"How do you mean, go on? It says wait while the green light operates." I peered down at the twenty-five-mile badge and noticed Jamie's face was angry and contorted. Behind me distant hooting and a lorry at my back was heavy-breathing with hydraulic brakes. The notice up in front was crude and painted by a workman probably. I mused about their spelling: 'opperates'.

"You've got to go!" His voice was strangled, choked. "Because it's green you've got to go. While means *until* in Yorkshire, don't you know?" His voice was full of scorn.

134

I let the clutch in slowly, heard him sigh, relax again. I still can't quite work out why I was wrong there at the traffic lights. Perhaps the man who had the proper notice was away today.

"And are you sure that nothing awful happened other than you missed the walk?" I was concerned about him now. He had become quite animated.

"I only mind about the traffic lights." He took another Mars bar from his pocket. "And things like that," he said.

The sun was high, but seemed to shine behind us. What time of day was this? We should be going south. Perhaps he had been lured into the walk-escaping jaunt: "Who else apart from you did not go on the twenty-five-mile walk?"

He said: "We're going wrong. This is the way to Pateley Bridge."

I might have said that we were going wrong in every walk of life, not just the twenty-five-mile one. Instead I slowed down, drew into a layby, waited till there was a gap in traffic and I took the road we had already come along. "We've wasted miles and miles and miles," said Jamie in disgust.

"There is a short-cut in a minute. Please be calm."

This narrow lane had verges grown head-high with bracken and pink campion. A couple in a gateway necking in a car, which Jamie turned to look at. Then he read the paper for a time. This road I knew. I'd cut this way before. You have to be a little careful that you bear round to the left. A lane down to the right leads to a reservoir. Keep on the level, going left and curving till you find the low bridge at the east end of the reservoir.

Jamie silent. "Tell me something from the paper then . . ."

"There is a new disease called something which I can't pronounce which can't be cured by penicillin any more. It sometimes seems things are quite like what Joel says they are."

Quite soon we'd meet the bridge and then climb up to reach the Roman road. A lack of signpost here confused. Jamie turned a page. A glimpse of water there beyond some trees. A forestry plantation this, with thick and bumpy lush green grass between young firs. A gate ahead. "I don't remember that this road was gated. Jamie—you will have to get out, open it."

Jamie said: "This is the gate into the reservoir. It's locked. Look! There's the notice!"

"That only says it's private fishing here."

He got out, stood beside the gate. He might have been a teacher pointing at the letters on a blackboard. He mouthed at me and shouted: "Yorkshire Water Board. Authorised Personnel Only."

I turned the engine off to save the petrol in the tank. The fuel gauge had been low throughout the journey. Now a light flashed on the dashboard.

A hostile place to be beleaguered this. The fir trees looked a limish sickly green. I noticed that the sky was grey. Why not get stuck in grassy glades instead of here beside an iron and wired-up gate and stony banks on either side. The wind got up and caught the tops of trees.

I'd walked this way before. With Jamie too, and Clo. When James, before he took up sport in earnest, said the thing to do was walk together in the countryside, and bought a dozen books of mapped-out tracks. We'd follow rivers to their source, regardless of the obstacles. We had new boots. He carried Jamie on his back. Clo whined about the weight of her boots. James carried Jamie on his back and disappeared into the mist. I cried with the weight of boots as well, and thoughts of Joel, and hung behind with Clo. We did not go again.

James walked the Dales alone and encumbered after that, from Kettlewell to Ingleborough, from Malham Cove to Pennyghent and up and down assorted peaks. Not far enough to shake the dust of nuclear unrest in the family.

This time I went in front with Jamie far behind, plodding up the hill with empty can. And at the top I waited in the gateway where we'd seen that couple kiss. Jamie caught me up and pulled a can of beer out of his pocket. "But you don't like beer."

"I do now," and he offered me a drink.

Our progress was a little quicker once the beer can had been emptied, thrown away, and once we'd eaten all the Mars bars in his rucksack. But the wind came down into our faces, grey and dry.

"The man who ran the camp was in the National Front," said Jamie in the gateway as he threw the empty beer can into the rubbish bin.

"Oh darling, no. You must have meant the National Trust."

Tear of rage glistened in his eyes. "It *was* the National Front."

"Oh very well," I said. "It was the National Front."

Friday: p.m.

So Friday night was party night at Ron and Barbara's. We went in round the front and were not an unimpressive group. Joel had put his best blue trousers on and a white shirt, very plain. At my suggestion he had added something silver—a medallion to demonstrate we'd not forgotten what importance the occasion signified. Bruce had his near-white trousers on and a green silk shirt his other auntie had sent from Adelaide. I, having lost weight what with all the worry of the week, was able to slip on the white silk dress, chemise in style, I last wore when we went to hear Ted Hughes at Ilkley quite some time ago. One cannot hope to look as grand as Ron and Barbara's friends who favoured lamé, velvet, silk and always shoes of silver or of gold.

Ron flung wide the door and greeted us like long-lost friends who had trekked across the desert to be with him. He was quite resplendent in a ruffled shirt and red bow tie. He'd been to have his hair blow-waved and flashed today. He looked like Charlton Heston in a way. Their Ashley too was no less smart in velvet breeches to the knee and polished cowboy boots. Lorraine was by his side as sweet and scented as you might expect from one who holds Boots' top sales assistant prize, and she was wearing Ashley's ring.

The room was crowded. All the usual guests were there: Pete and Carol from the Edna's, Jock and Mabel who have a do-it-yourself shop down our main street, Jim and Annie who come all the way from Bradford for one of Ron and Barbara's do's (Jim is a probation officer and Annie has a boutique), Sandra and Geoff who are reputed to be millionaires; they own a local take-away pizza shop and most take-away pizza shops between here and Halifax. And many others, glowing luxuriously dressed and sunburnt from the Balearic Isles. And not forgetting Sid the pathologist with whom Ron got on friendly terms the time he had his gallstones out.

Relations, too, of course: Ron's brothers who are less good-looking than he is; Ron's sister and her husband who's in ICI. I wondered if the uncle who'd attempted suicide was here.

I took my drink and focused on a table laden with a hundred shiny bottles: Campari and Martini, vodka and Baccardi, ranks of Coke and lemonade and tonic, two enormous thermos bowls, both crammed with ice and each with silver-plated tongs to lift the cubes and drop them tinkling into glasses.

I found a corner of their long four-seater couch and sat back with my drink, with Joel beside me. We were a little late and had some drinking to catch up with. Joel kept me company although there was no need for this. He was in an expansive mood. For Joel believes that all this wealth surrounding us is earned, deserved, and we should share in their enjoyment of their wealth. He held my hand because of his enjoyment. It seemed that we were reconciled. I held his hand and took it that we were. I urged him to go off and join in all the silver wedding jokes which echoed round the room, jokes of the nature: "Well, you'll have had it twenty-five times, Ron!"

And Ron, replying, "Aye—you could say that!" or sometimes, "I should be so lucky!"—all that sort of thing.

"Go on," I said to Joel. He is so good at parties. Parties bring the colour to his cheeks and draw from him a bonhomie which is remarkable in one so plagued by doubts. He loves to please his hosts and make it worth their while to have invested in his beer. He gives more pleasure, to my mind, than any alcohol. The principle is one of fair return, but with great warmth and vigour. His repertoire of jokes exeeds in number the poems he has written, his store of anecdotes is inexhaustible. I'm glad to have the chance of showing Joel the way he was that night, at least the way he was when first he left my side and soon became the centre of a laughing crowd. And soon I'd go and dance with him. Not on my own as at the Ivy.

My legs were aching from the walk I'd done, but soon I'd dance. I'd have to go and check that Jamie was all right next door alone, but soon I'd dance.

And Bruce as well was happy and relaxed. It seemed he had forgiven me my most unjust remark of Thursday night. The plaster just above his eye gave him a somewhat dashing look. I watched him as he mingled with the guests and nudged and joked like Joel. The surging sound from speakers round the room, the lustre of the clothes and drinks, rich textures I embraced and felt enjoyment creeping up on me. Though something was forgotten, wasn't it? The envelope I should have passed to Bruce had slipped out of the pocket of my jeans, perhaps back there beside the reservoir. I'd have to pass the message on by spoken word, by Christ I would.

Soon drink began to numb my mind. Beside me now was Ron. He leaned back, kissed me. People all around us laughed and nudged each other, saying, "That's the way for silver weddings, is it then?"

"Is everything all right?" I said to Ron.

"It's great, it's great," said Ron. "Now don't you worry now!"

"I would have written you a silver wedding ode," I said, "but somehow I have lost the muse this week . . ."

I sat there holding Ron's warm hand and fantasised that he and I were in a little house together on our own and all I had to do was add his takings up at night and calculate the VAT and listen to the stories that he read from history books and learn that there was nothing new or worse that people did today than they had ever done. Amidst the throng of people and the music and the smoke, the woes and burdens, thoughts of envelopes and Clo all fell away and crawled among the shining shoes and dwindled on the inch-thick carpeting. And Joel came up and said, "Now is this good or is this good?"—a way he had not spoken for, it seemed, a year. He danced away again, his arms above his head, thumbs clicking like a Spanish dancer.

When Gerry first came in I thought of getting up and going up to him, but I was talking to a vicar at the time, discussing ritual. From this we somehow turned to T. S. Eliot, on whom (I was a little miffed to find) he was on safer ground than I, and so I steered the conversation round to Ron and Barbara whom he married twenty-five years back. But that, the vicar said, reminded him how old he was. He changed the subject back to ecumenicism. His presence was distracting, stimulating, his intellect a challenge to a mind which had been dawdling in low gear for weeks. Nor was he old, I said I thought.

"They must have been your first—first wedding, Ron and Barbara must . . ."

I noted Gerry at the door, a little wild-eyed, dirty. His safari suit was very crumpled. But the vicar seemed to want to go on talking. He was gazing at my cleavage by that time and issuing an invitation that I go and read my poetry from his pulpit. He was a hefty parson with large hands and curly hair and bulging white silk shirt and I was pondering my choice of work and whether if I read in church I would be thus committing myself to something I'd rejected years ago. "Except the ritual—I love the psalms and that," I said, "and candles, all that sort of thing, and weddings in a way do have . . ." Strong presence at my shoulder over us. He looked distrait and somewhat menacing.

I'd also been thinking while I chatted to this man of God that I had often wondered if, in deep distress, one could just pop into St Jude's and prostrate, flattened out before the altar, arms outstretched, be humble and feel better afterwards without attacking Joel. For God, if he is there, must have illimitable and invulnerable ego, if he's male that is, and if he's not, then we'd be fighting equal as they say.

But Gerry, who as mentioned has a booming voice, was standing there above us saying: "So it's reading from the pulpit, is it now?"

141

I introduced him to the vicar, then said: "Hullo Gerry.
I say, where is Pru?"

The vicar looked up briefly, said to Gerry he was pleased
to meet him, then turned back to me, and Gerry did not
answer me nor did he tell me where Pru was. I hoped the
vicar would have heard of Gerry, but when I said "McLeHose"
he did not seem impressed. By then my mind was fast at work.
I knew that Gerry must at all costs straightway be included
in the conversation. For if he still was lapsed into his old-
iconoclastic mood, then he would leap upon this figure of
the old establishment and aim at high-speed shock. And so
I said: "Gerry is a poet, really *is* a poet . . ."

"I was. I was! Once was!" said Gerry, flopping down on
the far side of the vicar.

"You *are*! Of course you are," I said.

"Shit, Monica, I'm done for, and I haven't won the
Arsington Award."

"You might be second, Gerry, even third."

"Oh Christ!" said Gerry, covering his face with hands.
"Oh help me father for I've sinned." He turned to me. "I've
found out who the winner is."

Poor Gerry. He was quite beyond himself. The vicar showed
no signs of shock and went on talking of the Tannoy system
which he has in church and whether I would like the pulpit
or the lectern for my reading. So I said: "Excuse me, vicar.
I must get my friend a drink," and rose. I chose malt whisky
neat and dropped some ice cubes into it with Ron and
Barbara's silver-plated tongs. But Gerry'd gone when I
returned. The vicar said: "Your friend seems very troubled,
doesn't he?"

"He is in mid-life crisis."

The vicar nodded. "Feeling pretty useless then."

"It is the Grassington Award," I said, "and not the
Arsington."

"Ah, yes."

"It is for poetry. An open competition."

"He is lucky he has friends like you."

"You see to be a poet is like nothing else. It all comes from your head, and if your head is troubled . . ."

The vicar said that he had once wished that he might be a photographer, but soon discovered that he had not quite the knack. He used to do some water-colour painting, but he had to give that up. I did not like the way that he was drawing parallels between the art that Gerry practised and his own and probably amateurish efforts. And nor did Gerry, so it seemed, for he had come back now and sat between us, legs stuck out, his whisky in his hand and said: "Your Joel has won the fucking Arsington Award."

I looked around for Joel. His cup would overflow with joy; this was the news which would return us to the even tenure of our lives. "Where is he?" I was calling out. "Where is he? Have you told him, Gerry?" I so much wished to run and break the news myself.

A little trouble flared about that time, I am afraid. The cause was Bruce again, though once again poor Bruce was innocent. I'd tried to keep an eye on him. I'd hoped when I was drunk enough I'd have the guts to tell them that there'd been this envelope. But all was well as long as he was joking in the midst of other males. It did not seem that he would make approaches to the women there, excepting possibly Lorraine. Although it crossed my mind that since my accusation of impotency the night before, he might just feel the need to prove himself.

Poor Bruce. I watched him dancing with Lorraine, and she looked very starry-eyed and glowing with excitement as she threw herself around in very gay abandon with her skirt twirled up. And Ashley wasn't bothered on the whole. I think he watched with pride. Clean frilly knickers flashed and perfect tights. She wasn't even touching Bruce. He stamped and danced with flopping hair in that same private ecstasy I had experienced myself the night before, his pale blue eyes were clear against the bright green of his shirt, the sleeves of this rolled up, the light caught golden hairs upon his arms.

143

The music was *Viva L'Espagna* and there was nothing lusty in the steps Bruce took, except he did once put his index fingers to his head like horns and charge across the dancing space in imitation of a bull.

I was on my way across the room to Joel who also danced, but lightly in a kind of soulful way and with a woman in a low-cut tight black dress with bosoms bulging plum-like out of it.

Now Barbara had been busy, laughing, jolly in a way. She had a private grief, however; Nicola had not arrived. This fairest flower and brain, perhaps the real achievement of those twenty-five years, had sent a greetings telegram, but that was all.

Barbara was beside me now. She watched the way Lorraine was dancing. Then she took Ashley by the arm. I didn't hear exactly what she said, but Ashley in reply: "Oh no, Mum. That's all right! That's O.K., Mum. She's only dancing, Mum."

Barbara too has danced like that. I've seen her dance. In fact I said to her: "Oh come on, Barbara, the times I've seen you dance like that!"

Beside me also was Big Paul, the lad who had come up to me the night before, the one who shows his chest hair off and lives at number forty-six. He stood there like a mighty cowboy towering over all of us. I heard him say to Ashley: "He had better keep his hands off her. I've heard there's no one that he hasn't had round here," and then he added: "And we don't know what goes on in there!" His message was quite clear. He spoke of number forty-two, our house. He gestured, and his gesture must, I think, have been in my direction too, although I was surprised he even noticed me. I only reach his hirsute waist.

But Joel saw this, stopped dancing right away, and came towards us, fists and all. He broke away from dancing with the woman in the tight black dress, and there was in his face a look more war-like even than the look he'd had the night he castigated Friends of St Winifred's Old Folk's Club, more

144

fierce than when he told me not to patronise. No, nothing of
Il Penseroso now, but Joel on the warpath and about to strike
a blow, to break his rule of all-good-neighbours-everyone and
challenge someone taller than him by a head.

I don't know what I would have done, except to step and
take Joel's glasses off for him. I was about to do that very
thing, but Barbara got there first. She stood there stoutly,
strongly in her silver lamé top and swinging skirt, her hair a
halo. She was perfect and imposing: "No, none of that! I
won't have that! I've had enough of that last night. There
won't be any blood drawn here. As if you could, Joel
Trotter!"

I tried to shout: "Oh Barbara, no, that isn't fair! Poor
Joel!" I could not bear to look at him. He turned and pushed
back through the party people all surrounding him, and Bruce
who had stopped dancing and was ready, so it seemed, to line
up, rolled up sleeves and all, with Joel, looked most abashed
and caught Joel's arm and followed him, not through the
front door—not the way we came, but out through Barbara's
kitchen door and left me standing, shattered, wide-eyed, lost.
And should I follow him? I looked at Barbara desperately
and said: "I think I'll have to go as well."

"You please yourself," said Barbara. Murmurs, people
falling back. I left the room.

The scene was Barbara's kitchen now. Some guests had
overflowed in there, and dancing too—to speakers on the wall.
The shining floor, the bright brass fittings and the lamps
which hung above the gleaming sinks of stainless steel.

They hang all round the room, these lamps. They're
anodised, resembling brass, and Barbara has them since she
hates the striplight that she used to have. And thus the kitchen
is a series of light-pools upon the surfaces she uses to make
bread and cakes and other surfaces she uses to cut steak on,
dismember chickens. People moving in the centre of the floor
in shadow. Walnut units interspersed with white enamel of
her washer and her dishwasher.

The first impression was that Barbara had left red towels

145

piled upon the floor. And then I thought that someone must have spilled Martini or Campari there. And then I noticed red stains on the white front of her fridge. I made to go across the room and reach the outside door.

But all the red was blood. Not trickles of it like it came from Bruce's little wound, but splodges of it as if someone threw a bucket of it. Or rather as if someone with an aerosol of blood had gone around and sprayed it on the quarry tiles and white enamel.

It came from someone slumped against the sink and bending at the waist, and people seemed to stand around and look at him. Perhaps the wound from which the blood was flowing had been made but seconds since. Perhaps as I came in.

At first I thought it was a bloody nose and looked around for Bruce and Joel, but they had gone. And then I recognised the boots and saw that they were Maurice's. A knife was by the boots and pointing, messy-bladed, out along the floor towards a stool where young Lorraine was weeping and enfolded in her fiancé's arms.

It happened that I know where Barbara keeps her ironing-board and with it there's a sheet she spreads to keep her ironing clean. I pressed the button of a walnut door, the ironing-board sprang out. I grabbed the sheet and rushed to wrap it round his head, around the head and shaggy dripping hair and pushed him to the floor. He slid and where I knelt beside him there was slime of blood beneath my knees and soaking up my dress.

I think my first intent was to conceal the dreadful source of all the blood. When desperation strikes, the human body bursts and leaks, is burst or made to leak. He'd tried to do like poor Van Gogh, demented as he was, but hadn't managed that at all. I looked around the oozing puddles, marvelled at the thickness of the blood and prayed I would not see an ear.

I think that it was Gerry who had followed me, who went to fetch the thermos bowl of ice and piled it on the floor beside the head, then bound up ice cubes in a tea-cloth, held them there beside the wound. By that time other people

146

moved away towards the edges of the room and left just me and Maurice, Gerry too, me kneeling down. I lifted up the head. It could be said I cradled it. It was a *pieta* in a way. No tenderness intended though, but only that the quarry tiles were hard, and raising up the head might make it harder for the heart to pump blood to the wound. (In detail—and I learned it from the Irish sister at the hospital—Maurice had sliced one inch only into the bridge of skin which fastens lobe to head, a plentifully bleeding place but not by any means a fatal one.)

Then Ron was there. He stood a little back from us to keep his polished crocodile casuals free from bloody pools. He said, "She says you've got to get him out of here. She says it's got to be cleaned up. I'm sorry, love, but that is what she says ..." and through the open door I could see Barbara crying and surrounded by her friends.

The casualty ward is long and low, an annexe, airport-like. But we have been there, haven't we, this week? The Irish sister was on duty still. Not Terence Meadowcroft this time, but some young Indian person yawning with a brand new leather doctor's bag. I heard no sound from Maurice, but I heard the sister say: "That's it, my love; you wanted pain."

She wheeled him out again: "And this one's one you had by someone else, you will be telling me!" He, Maurice, looked like someone Frankenstein had not quite finished with —before the bandages were removed to see if the experiment had worked. And this time Gerry sat beside me waiting on an orange chair and drove us home.

I put him, Maurice, on the russet linen couch, a cushion for his swathed head. There was a musty smell which mixed with antiseptic smells. I did not touch his boots but left them on and hoped he was too weak to reach and take them off himself. And Gerry kept on saying that we should have left him there in hospital.

"If Clo can do it, I can too," I said, "but this time I will take him home."

147

Upstairs I stripped out of my white chemise silk dress and put it in the bath. Blood soaks away in water, but the water must be cold. I ran it out, pink water, and refilled it till it turned a paler pink. Rosé. I swirled the water round and round and saw red traces still emerging. Trails of smoke from planes shoot out like that and thin into the sky.

A kind of vigil in our brown armchair. It is the best place we can watch our TV from. It's also in the centre of the room, midway between the sitting and the kitchen end, and anyone who rose and went in search of knives, would surely have to pass the chair and wake the watcher up. Gerry stayed until he went in search of Joel, to tell Joel he had won the bardic crown of all the Ridings. "I'm sorry that you didn't win, and thanks," I said.

Before he left he put this cable through for me to James. CLO ON WAY VIA HITCHHIKE. PLEASE REPORT ARRIVAL URGENT then rephrased it for me patiently: URGENT CLO ON WAY VIA HITCHHIKE STOP PLEASE REPORT ARRIVAL VERY URGENT. And found for me, in case I needed it, the number of the British Consul in St Malo.

Saturday

There are some people you are loth to touch. When Clo was little I would take her to my cleaning lady once a week so I could go and shop. The cleaning lady lived in what they called a scullery house in Leeds. It smelt of heaters fuelled by oil and last night's stew. When Clo came home—I fetched her—I would bathe and scrub the whole of her and swear I'd never send her there again, clean every particle of her and sterilise all evidence of where she'd crawled and staggered.

I could not clean her now. I could not clean him, Maurice, either. But I woke him up and edged him out towards the car, the front door way. And on the mat there was a letter which I bent, picked up. It was from Clo, the one she said she'd sent to tell me all.

I knew he lived in Rotherham, or that was where his mother lived, but had to trust that he would tell me where to go. We could not leave until the petrol stations opened, which was why I found the letter there. I'd meant to go at dawn.

The M1 stretched before us now and sunny streams of weekend traffic hurtling north and south with loaded roof racks, cars with couples in, their names on windscreens: Dave and Sandra. Michael and Louise. Behind me in the middle lane I read in mirror image John and Caroline.

You see [wrote Clo] I think it's in perspective now. At least I thought it was. I'm sorry that I haven't said before what happened. I kept on thinking things would be all right again. And then they weren't. He said I didn't love him. Well, I didn't maybe quite so much by then, but went on saying that I did. I'm writing this at night. I'm baby-sitting. Keith and Nina have gone out. I said about the

149

twins I think. I realise now I'm O.K. if I am with someone.
Anyone. If I'm alone I think I hear him coming. I thought
it would be different when we went away. It was all right
to start with. Up to Glastonbury. But we met Keith and
he tried to help and didn't take my side a lot. But Maurice
thought he did.

You get used to the blood. You learn to hide the pills.
You learn to hold him off. You *know* he can be nice. You
know it's just an ego trip for him and he is using you.
You *know* he'd never do it, not for real.

I should have told you months ago. About the time of
Bruce. It started after that. And all the times he'd done it
with my friends! I thought what bloody sauce!

The funny thing—I miss him. Well, I just miss having
someone, though the twins help. It is super here. It really
is. We take the twins down to the beach. The pools are
lukewarm. You have to watch them all the time—the twins.
Their names are Lee and Lucy. Lee has very curly hair
and Lucy's is quite straight and black. She looks a bit
Chinese. They're not identical.

But I can see in winter that it could be awful. Scary. I
can see why gunge is on the roof. There is a gale. Don't
worry. I won't go unless it's calm. You feel the roof lift up
and when it rains you have to roll up towels and put them
on the window sill . . .

Then Maurice came out of the gents and we set out again
for Rotherham. He told me how to go. But often he said
"Turn left" after we had passed the turning, so I'd stop and
back the car.

The house was terrace in a street with gardens at the far
end. But no trees. A man with tattoos on his face was standing
on a corner and he peered into the car.

I'm sure it's often sunny there in Rotherham, but the sun
seemed dimmed as we left the M1 and cloud hung low in
front of us. Maybe we were running into promised storms.
The terrace houses in the street were grey and there were

150

cobbles, and you couldn't drive up to the house because there were iron bollards at one end. It was a safe-play street I think. Washing hung across. I have seen streets like that before, the one where I used to take Clo when I left her with the cleaning lady.

I took him by the hand. We'd parked the car beside the bollards at the end. I was quite used by then to holding on to Maurice, used to the musty smell relieved by antiseptic. I was surprised, to tell the truth, he hadn't needed a transfusion after all that blood. But blood renews itself, the sister said. A pint is nothing; you can give a pint, recover with a cup of tea. I tried to calculate. Perhaps he'd lost two pints.

I thought it would be just my luck if Mum was out. I had asked Maurice if she worked on Saturdays. He said she cleaned for people weekdays, cleaned for a lady out on Sheffield Road. He said she'd always cleaned for her and when he was a little boy he used to go and polish things as well. That was about the only thing he talked about at all. We drove in silence mostly. And Jamie was alone at home which agitated me as much as anything.

Michel thinks we can go on Friday and I hope I will have heard from you by then. I've got the PC with the French address. Can't wait to meet Françoise. Don't worry. I am in one piece and will be home . . .

We'd stopped once along the motorway. I sat there in a service station with the window open, reading Clo's letter. It was a woody place that looks down on South Yorkshire mines and hills and railway lines. The sun was falling on the trees around the car park and people crossed in front of me to go into the café and the shop.

We'd also stopped in Leeds one time. Perhaps it was from nerves. He was about to see his Mum and hadn't seen her for some time. Or maybe it was all the hot sweet tea I'd given him. And I could only sit there in the car and hope he wouldn't cut his wrists or anywhere inside the gents. He hadn't anything to cut things with. I did not take him to his flat to fetch his things, believing I might not get him out of there again.

For all I knew the address in Rotherham was a fiction. I thought of that when waiting at the service station. Clo wrote:

... perhaps I shouldn't have expected help from Keith, although he shared our tent and helped me talk Maurice through the night. That's all. But all the same it meant that Maurice wouldn't sleep in case. We had to drink a lot with him because that sometimes calms him down. And by the way I didn't just walk out with Keith and leave him—Maurice—on his own. There were some other people in the next tent who were very understanding and they said they'd cope ...

It must have been the right house since he didn't knock but took the handle, pushed it inwards and we stood inside the lino-shiny hall and smelt the smell of boiling clothes.

His mother: I should say what she was like. Clo, having been there once or twice, had told me that she was small, thin and very lively. Perhaps she's best described that way. Eyes full of hope at any rate as she dried her hands and put her arms around him, only reaching to his shoulder. He bent down. His hair hung down around her face—at least the left side did; the right side had been cut back and was covered with the bandage.

She saw the bandage, did not flinch, but stood back and her bright eyes shifted from excitement at his visit to alarm. The only way to make this clear is to say *before* they had been dancing with the pleasure of his presence while the *after* view was that they seemed receded, seemed to go back in her head.

I think she shook my hand: "Clo's Mum is very welcome here," or maybe it was that she said: "Clo's Mummy's very welcome here," and bustled us into a room, the door of which was shut, but which she opened, made us go in there. The best room, full of photographs of Maurice as a little boy, at

152

which I didn't want to look but had to in the end in order to make conversation. Although the case must surely be that conversation on occasions of that kind is quite superfluous and inappropriate. In fact I had decided I would make none. I was on a mission of a most unsocial kind.

There was a piano and a piano stool and Maurice sat there on the stool and sagged as he had all the morning, staring into space. He looked like some great lanky half-unfeathered bird on a perch. While everything around was clean and shiny. All the shelves had brass-type curly edging, high polished, varnished maybe. Pot plants grew along the shelves and there were special metal fixtures on the wall to let them curl around. They flourished, grew up into corners of the room, across the ceiling, down the chandelier.

She had done well with plants. A school report might say: 'Done well with plants but not with son', at whom she gazed with loving warmth from time to time. If he was like a large bird on the piano stool, then she was like a robin. Perhaps I choose the robin since she had a reddish sweater on, red nylon trousers underneath her apron which was brown, and small neat feet.

And I was Mrs Crossley, which I'm not of course, but it seemed silly to explain, and she was Mrs Brett and we were like I'd just come round for tea and chat, and was it fine today where I came from? And what a summer it had been. She and Frank were off to Bridlington. But every now and then she looked at Maurice, and with warm and scolding voice said something like, "Oh love, you should have told me, lovey, yes you should," and leaning forward put her hand on his and clicked her tongue. You couldn't fault her warmth. Where does warmth get you, though, I thought?

Between all this, and helpless, I discovered I was making what might just be called admiring noises at the plants and knew the name of one—a hoya—but it seems to me you can't go into someone's room where vegetation's bursting and a deal of skill has been employed to nurture it and not say, "But how lovely!" can you?

I should have said, "Look, Mrs Thing, your son has fucked my life up all this week and fucked my daughter up for years maybe, and as for what he's done self-wise I wouldn't like to say and hardly care."

Instead I said: "And do you feed them biograd?"

And she said things like: "And Clo, is she on holiday abroad? How lovely for her! Such a lovely girl!"

I should have said: "Now, Mrs Thing, just get your apron off and take him off and get his head turned inside out. Don't leave him for a minute. Get him out there in the garden at the back, if you have one and I'm sure you do, and tell his Dad when he comes home that he has got to take the lad and . . ." Instead of which I let her put a posh voice on for me and let her tell me of the holidays they'd had in Scotland and the Isle of Man and point out coloured snap-shots which showed little Maurice on the sands or little Maurice in a bumper car or little Maurice eating pink ice cream, and there was slightly bigger Maurice on his first new bike, this bike in colour red. The print had faded. Even if his bike was brilliant red when new, his blood is redder than his bike.

And when I left she put her hands up on his shoulders, leaned towards me round his body and she said: "I'll see to everything; don't worry. Have a nice drive back and love to Clo!"

I had just mentioned in a low and most embarrassed voice that he had stitches to come out a week from now.

"She's five foot three or four, has dark hair, rather curly and wears jeans, and when I say she's on her way to Perpignan, it's rather complicated why. Yes—definitely St Malo was their landfall and I thought you might have heard if any fishing boats . . ."

It wasn't hard to ring the British Consul at St Malo. I had the number Gerry'd copied out for me. The British Consul was about to go to lunch. He was about to shut the office up for the weekend, he said. I said I was surprised he closed the office at weekends because that surely was a time when many English people might get lost or ill or short of francs and other things they go to British Consuls for. But it was lucky that I rung him then before he went to lunch. The call, made from the M1 service station, was expensive.

He was most polite and patient on the whole, considering that I could only name the boat and state its colour and design, the first name of its owner, if he *was* its owner, where it had arrived from, fairly patient on the whole.

"But could you maybe, or your secretary, if you have one— I know it's just about to be the weekend—but all the same, she's quite distinctive—no, I mean my daughter is distinctive, not your secretary, and walks with confidence, my daughter and, if she's pleased with life, she sort of swaggers, moves her shoulders rather more than some. I don't know if she's pleased with life just now, I'm afraid. She might be, though. I don't know either if there would be someone with her, possibly this Michel. I think she said he had broad shoulders, a moustache, was very vir . . . very bronzed, but definitely, the ship, the boat was called *Mon Rêve* . . ."

It seemed there isn't just one fishing harbour at St Malo, but at least three choices where a boat might moor. But all the same I'd done what I could, and Clo will maybe know one day I'd done it all. He sounded nice enough, the British Consul did, and had, which I had not expected, a broad West Country accent.

I got back in the car, was up there on the motorway again. The sun was out and hot and as I crossed the tarmac, cars poured in and out again. I fastened up the safety belt and headed home.

The Avenue looked odd right from the moment that I turned the corner out of Phyllis Road. I cannot work out yet exactly what it was that seemed so untoward. Or maybe it was Barbara standing there outside her door and looking at me as I stopped the car. Not Jamie was it? Could he now be bleeding since it seemed that blood was in the air this week.

155

High noon, I thought, and got out of the car. "Has Joel come back?" I said because I could not bear to ask how Jamie was. I reached her front gate, held the gatepost rather as I'd held the pillar of our banisters that night I thought that Maurice was downstairs and creeping up on me.

"I wouldn't know," she said.

She stood back and made way for me. It seemed I had to go inside. The room was clean, no sign of party evidence, no crumbs, no ash, no bottles, but the clean sweep of her carpet and the leather three-piece suite, and Jamie sitting there, a glazed look in his eyes: "What happened, Barbara?"

"Well, nothing much you could say in one sense," she shook her hand. She had been putting on nail varnish. "Or you could say quite a lot."

"And Bruce," said Jamie, "has gone in search of Clo. He says he wants to marry her."

"Now don't be silly, darling, please. He's much too young to settle down, and so is she." I looked across the wide expanse of Barbara's room and through the picture window at the end and saw their blue and white umbrellas moving slightly in the wind. "I don't know, though. They might as well." By which time Jamie had begun to laugh. His head down between his knees, then up again and thrown against the back of Barbara's leather couch. Another kind of tears were in his eyes.

"Lorraine has broken off her engagement," Barbara said.

"But what has that to do with it?" I said.

"Look, here's the ring." She picked it from a glass dish on the mantelpiece and held it out. She put it on her little finger, waved her hand around. It slipped and fell on to the carpet. Then she picked it up again and handed it to me. "You have it. Bruce can get engaged to Clo with that. Lorraine's decided she's too young to settle down."

"The silly girl," I said, and gave it back.

Then Jamie stood up, ran out of the room. I heard him shut the door of Barbara's downstairs lavatory. "He has been sick already twice," she said.

I couldn't say exactly why he chose to open up the turnip wine. That will emerge in due course when there's time to think about it. There is also getting passport photos taken, finding birth certificate with which to get the passport. There is ringing up the airline, finding where he has to change in Paris, whether he will be escorted through the airport as he changes planes. They keep an eye on kids in planes, as Clo said just the other day.

I left him and drove away at speed, but haunted by the look on Barbara's face as well as that on his. I drove as Barbara drove on Thursday night but over hills and down again to Grassington. No cosmic feelings such as Pru described, but as I said to Pru, when all is said and done, the Vatman paid and blood mopped up, the man you need to be with is the thing you drive towards, the man who fits, with whom you've made the contract willingly, without whom you would have no drive to drive. Blind panic grew. Perhaps I'd left it all too late, and if Joel had not got today some tribute to good art, he would have walked away again.

I drove and had this vision of the vicar that I met last night, a wedding there beneath his Gothic Arch, of Clo in white and Bruce in white as well maybe, and music booming out and Joel the other side of Clo. But then it wouldn't be Joel, would it? It would be James, but that would be all right, the Crossleys briefly reunited singing Love Divine. And afterwards, not at the Lamb and Flag perhaps, but somewhere with more room for all the guests, our multitude of friends— I'd stand and shake them by the hand and smile a little wanly saying: "Yes, they're much too young to settle down, but we will see—and yes, it was a lovely wedding, wasn't it, and yes, who knows, it might just last for long enough to bring a child or two to grow up wondering what hit them when they wake one morning, climb into their mother's bed and find strange flesh which has not got their blood in it." Joel came towards me down the platform steps, his cheque held high, his arms stretched out . . .

As Pru once pointed out, when she'd been reading *Antony*

157

and Cleopatra for a good quotation for a novel title, it always seemed to her they made love best when Antony had won a battle or was setting out in confidence for one.

Today is Sunday: James rang up. "Clo has not turned up yet," he said.

"I see."

"She's very vague you know."

"I do know that."

"Remember when she hitched back in that truck because we hadn't collected her from Youth Club all those years ago."

"I don't remember that."

On Sundays sometimes we have gatherings of friends. But not this Sunday though.